'Put me down ragged and ab

'Ain't gonna happen, he said, heiting her higher, closer. Her head tipped backwards as she gulped in much-needed air.

When she found the strength to pull her head upright once more, she looked right into his eyes. So dark and infinitely deep. And completely enraptured by her. *Her.* Somehow she wasn't completely terrified by all that blatant need. Because she trusted him.

To do what? Take her to heaven? Treat her right? Never hurt her? She shook her messy tumbling hair away from her face and shook herself free of those insidious thoughts. This wasn't about trust. This was about getting his naked skin on hers.

Dear Reader

I'll admit it. I am a chocoholic. My tastes in chocolate are broad and pretty much indiscriminate. But there is only one other sweet that has the potential to make me switch sides. And that is gelato.

Great glistening slabs of ice-cold *baci* and cinnamon-flavoured gelato piled high into a crunchy, sugary waffle cone. It can be the hottest Melbourne summer day, or so cold out that a person needs gloves and eight layers of clothing in order to leave the house. It doesn't matter. A gelato fix can never be denied. My mouth is watering and my right foot is tapping impatiently against the floor just thinking about it!

So when I had the idea for a simply gorgeous hero whose family owned a chain of mega-successful gelatarias, the notion stuck. Easily. No arguments from me. Spending months living deep inside a romantic, sexy love story is a wonderful way to make a living. Add gelato, and I'm surprised I was ever convinced to let the book go! Seriously, could a girl have a better job?

Any other gelato-lovers out there, feel free to contact me at ally@allyblake.com, or swing by my website for more sweet temptations.

Lotsa love

Ally

www.allyblake.com

STEAMY SURRENDER

BY
ALLY BLAKE

🌹™ **MILLS & BOON**®

Pure reading pleasure

All the characters in this book have no existence outside the imagination of the author, and have no relation whatsoever to anyone bearing the same name or names. They are not even distantly inspired by any individual known or unknown to the author, and all the incidents are pure invention.

First published in Great Britain 2007
Harlequin Mills & Boon Limited,
Eton House, 18-24 Paradise Road, Richmond, Surrey TW9 1SR

© Ally Blake 2007

ISBN: 978 0 263 85396 4

Set in Times Roman 10½ on 12¼ pt
171-0907-57830

Printed and bound in Spain
by Litografia Rosés, S.A., Barcelona

When **Ally Blake** was a little girl she made a wish that when she turned twenty-six she would marry an Italian two years older than her. After it actually came true she realised she was onto something with these wish things. So, next she wished that she could make a living spending her days in her pyjamas, eating M&Ms and drinking scads of coffee while turning her formative experiences of wallowing in teenage crushes and romantic movies into creating love stories of her own. The fact that she is now able to spend her spare time searching the internet for pictures of handsome guys for research purposes is merely a bonus!

Come along and visit her website at www.allyblake.com

Out next month in Mills & Boon® Romance
MILLIONAIRE TO THE RESCUE
Ally Blake's next book!

This one's for Paul and for Luke—
material proof there are good men out there
for the girls lucky enough to find them.

CHAPTER ONE

MORGAN pushed her large sunnies higher onto her nose, then stared across Como Avenue, the ice-cold Melbourne Street in which the cabbie had left her. She rubbed fast hands down her arms to ward off the insidious chill in the air. And she frowned. *This* was the reason she had spent twenty-four hours seated on planes, fifteen of those hours next to a guy who hadn't showered in at least a week?

When lawyers had contacted her in Paris less than two weeks earlier with the news that she'd inherited five shopfronts in Carlton, she'd been silly enough to allow herself to imagine a quaint florist, a charming café, maybe even a funky boutique or two.

But considering the bequest had come from her grandfather on her mother's side she ought to have known better. The Kiplings had two great talents: self-preservation, and intra-family disharmony. Passing on prime real estate in a move of last-minute conciliation would just have been out of character.

As it turned out, her inheritance offered a dry-cleaner, a real-estate agency with faded advertisements lining a cracked window, an Indian restaurant with dusty red curtains and crazed vinyl chairs haphazardly lining the footpath, and a place called Jan's Wool and Fabric with a sign so old it was missing the tenth digit that had been added to all Australian phone numbers many years before.

The final shopfront was the building's saving grace. With new signage, golden down-lights and clean windows, the façade of the Bacio Bacio Gelataria was like a sunburst of panache within the hotchpotch of ancient, dilapidated outlets. And though the idea of gelato seemed ludicrous considering it was at most five degrees outside, it was enough for Morgan to decide to start her stealthy reconnaissance there.

She stamped her half-numb feet against the cold, cracked concrete, took a gulp of her lukewarm, over-baked, congealing take-away coffee for courage, and checked the street before crossing, reminding herself to look right first and last. Yet while nearby Lygon Street hummed with constant traffic, Como Avenue had none.

'You sure ain't in Paris any more,' she told herself before jogging across the empty road.

Saxon sang along with his favourite CD as he turned Bessie, his beloved midnight-blue nineteen sixty-eight MkII Jaguar, off Lygon Street and into Como Avenue.

When she purred to a full stop in the staff parking area at the back of the run of shops, he gave her his habitual loving stroke of the dash, and told her what a good girl she was before getting out.

'Sheesh,' he said to no one in particular when the freezing wind whipped about his face and leached through his jeans.

He didn't remember it having been this cold in

years. Not since the halcyon days of cruising Lygon Street in nothing warmer than a T-shirt and Levi's 501s, the tape player in his hotted-up Monaro cranked loud with Billy Joel while his similarly under-dressed cousins shouted offers to the lucky ladies on the sidewalk as they thundered by.

He pulled his beanie tighter over his ears and his sheepskin collar higher around his neck. Not all was lost. The sky was crystal-clear indicating fresh snowfall on the northern mountaintops. He might still get the chance to take Bessie for a run up to Mount Buller before the week was out. Skiing, mulled wine by the open fire, some chilled-out music on the CD player. If he played his cards right, perhaps even a warm, willing ski bunny in faux fur and tight pants might help take the edge off.

The sound of a distant tinkling bell split the air, drawing him out of his daydream. He'd know the sound of that particular bell anywhere. For him it meant business.

He popped a stick of cinnamon gum in his mouth, waiting for the peppery sweetness to warm him as he jogged to the back door of the shop. He knew he ought to just give his cousin Darius his weekly kick in the pants and leave Trisha to handle the customers. But the thrill of the chase warmed his blood more than any Billy Joel song ever had.

Nope. Darius wouldn't get much of a wave before he spent a busy lunch hour doing what he did best. Selling ice cream even in the middle of winter.

The soft tinkling of an old-fashioned brass bell heralded Morgan's introduction to the Bacio Bacio Gelataria.

She slid her knee-length knitted scarf from around her neck and tied it around the handle of her oversized designer bag—one of a trillion freebies she received as a perk of working as a photographic set designer for a top fashion magazine in Paris. Then she strolled deeper into the room, her creative eye skimming over numerous visual delights.

Rendered walls were painted a deep golden yellow bar one feature wall covered in an impression of Tuscan hills. A huge gleaming bronze espresso machine took up a tidy portion of the long mahogany counter top, leaving the remainder of the space for curved glass cabinets, cleverly backlit to make the most of at least three dozen long trays filled with towering swirls of multi-coloured gelato, flat spoons sticking out the top of each mound like the first flag on Mount Everest.

It was the kind of place someone in her job dreamed of stumbling upon. A perfect blend of colour, texture and lighting. It bombarded the senses in such a way it sold not just foodstuffs, but an image, a feeling. She could imagine men in fedoras crowded around the several tiled wrought-iron tables talking football spreads, and little kids in newsboy caps sticking their noses against the large window, wishing they hadn't spent the last of their pocket money on some silly toy.

It was a pity she was here on not nearly so pleasant a task as scouting out a *Chic* magazine set. A great pity. Instead, by the end of the week she would have to have made a decision: up the rent astronomically to make the place viable, or sign off on the plans burning a hole in her bag and raze the building to the ground.

* * *

Once inside, Saxon replaced his beanie for a black
Bacio Bacio cap, left his leather jacket over a chair in
the staff room, and tied a deep red apron around his
waist, tightening the knot in front.

He tucked his hair behind his ears, decided he'd better
get a haircut before his mother saw him again, and then
hastened out into the warm, inviting surrounds of his
home away from home to find a woman had entered his
haven.

He slowed. For this was not just any woman, but a
woman who deserved a second glance. And a third.
And dinner and a movie and at least an attempt at a
nightcap.

Blonde she was. Dirty blonde with luscious waves
trailing long down her front. Huge dark sunglasses
covered half her small face. At least three gold chains
hung around her slim neck, carrying oversized charms
that jingled against one another as she moved through
the room, giving her a kind of musical quality. And
poking out from her ridiculously high-heeled bronze
sandals the nails of her dainty toes were painted
working-girl red.

Actually she was kind of small all over; the class of
woman his father would say fitted nicely into one's
pocket. Her pint-sized loveliness was sheathed in a tight
gold V-neck top that adhered lovingly to some seriously eye-catching curves, like caramel sauce over ice
cream. And a now-you-see-it-now-you-don't sliver of
skin between the bottom of her top and the top of calf-
length cargo pants kept him riveted for a good thirty
seconds.

Saxon made a concerted effort to rein in his libido,
which had become overexcited astonishingly quickly

for such a cold winter morning. For simmering just
below the initial wham-bam-thank-you-ma'am attraction he felt a thread of residual discomfort, like a red
flag waving in the very corner of his subconscious.
Something about this woman was making him itch.

He caught Trisha's eye instead and motioned that
he'd get this one. The grin on Trisha's face told him
she'd been more than half expecting it. He curled his
lip and it only made her giggle behind her hand before
she snuck out the back to take her morning break before
the lunch rush set in.

Alone with the mystery woman Saxon leaned on the
counter and began his signature pitch that had sold a
million gelatos and turned his family's one small
suburban shop into a trans-Tasman empire.

'What's your poison?' he asked.

The woman's head tilted his way, and she regarded
him silently for a few moments.

Just like that his itch grew, and spread. Fast and
furious. Sudden and stunning. Like chicken pox, or
sunburn, or bad news. He had no idea if it was caused
by her lack of the usual childlike smile that people wore
when entering one of his establishments, the fact that
she was carrying a cup of a competitor's coffee, or that
he couldn't see her eyes behind her huge black sunglasses.

As though she knew just what he was thinking, the
woman reached up and lifted her sunglasses atop her
head, pulling her dirty blonde waves away from her
elfin face. And anything else Saxon might have been
about to say, or think, dried up as he looked into the most
stunning eyes he'd ever seen. *Ever.* In his *entire* life.

True green eyes in his experience were mostly a

fallacy. A way of prettying up hazel. Of explaining multicoloured flecks that damped down pure blues. But this woman's eyes were the colour of lush summer grass.

Fine eyes, fine backsides and fine senses of humour had proven his undoing on more than one occasion. If she bent over and told a joke he was afraid he might just ask her to marry him on the spot.

She took her time giving him a once-over easily as detailed as his own had been. Trailing over his too-long hair, his three-day growth, his favourite short-sleeved black T-shirt.

It was then that he realised that she was not in fact salivating over his stock. In any sense of the word. While his babe radar was on high alert. Sirens blaring. Spotlights ablaze and pointing her way. As he promptly found himself deep in the fantasy of her lying back on the sheepskin rug in front of the roaring fire at his Mt Buller cabin wearing nothing but a mink bikini, those luscious green eyes turning a deep, dense jade as he set to proving how superior his merchandise was.

His itch grew until he actually had to scratch his arm. He was beginning to think it was an early warning sign honed by having gone through a messy marriage and an even messier divorce, all of which made him highly aware of his own lack of rational romantic instincts.

'What's good here?' she asked.

It was simply too good a line to leave be. Itch or no itch. He held both arms wide to take in the whole shop. '*Everything* here will be the best you've ever had.'

Morgan laughed. Out loud. For she had no doubt the guy behind the counter had included himself in that statement. *Cocky as well as cute*, she thought. Though she only said, 'That's quite some claim.'

He placed a hand over his heart. Long fingers splayed out across a wall of cotton-clad muscle. 'I back it up with my own personal guarantee.'

'Brave business practice.'

'Bravery suggests doubt. I've simply never had any complaints.' His smile slid easily into a grin, all strong cheekbones and creased eyes and light-handed persuasion.

Morgan cleared her throat and trained her expression back towards ambivalent politeness. She was here to case the joint. Not to admire the guy at the counter. 'I'll take your word for it.'

She did what she should have done far earlier and moved away from him and further down the counter. For this was meant to be a quick look. In and out. Make a decision. Go home to Paris. To her cosy Montmartre apartment with its wrought-iron balcony big enough to fit only one smallish person, but positioned just so that she was afforded a sliver view of the exquisite splendour of Sacre Coeur, a building her father had promised would make her heart ache it was so beautiful. And it did, meaning her fourteen-hour days making tolerable money whoring her talents for Alicia, the world's least tasteful magazine editor, were all worth it.

The *in* had happened but the *out* part seemed to have hit a snag. For the moment her eyes had met a pair of dashing dark brown counterparts she'd felt…peculiar. Not bad peculiar. But funny-in-the-tummy peculiar. As if she'd had too much coffee. But considering the congealing latte in her hand hadn't deserved the three sips she'd afforded it…

Okay, maybe, just maybe, the peculiar feeling had

nothing to do with milk overload. Maybe it had everything to do with the fact that the guy was the most
overtly male person she had ever laid eyes on. Even
though he was blokey; no doubt the type who roved in
a pack and thought calling out to a woman that she had
a nice butt was commensurate to a first date, he was also
just so…big. Tall and broad. A silver chain clung tight
to his solid neck, allowing a small medallion to rest in
the dip in his clavicle. Smooth, tightly bound arm
muscles strained under a dark T-shirt advertising a rock
band she was fairly sure had broken up before she was
even born. They were the kind of muscles that made her
want to reach out and touch. And she just knew his
stomach would be washboard flat. And rippled. The
potential for ripples was super high.

All that healthy, robust manliness was something if
she really thought about it. Especially when compared
with the overly thin, overly coiffed, overly effeminate
types she worked with every day. And she was thinking
about it. Quite a lot.

She risked a sideways glance at the guy to find he
was watching her and she had to hold a hand over her
stomach to quell the sudden strange, bouncy, uncalled-
for butterflies within. No matter what kind of peculiar
she felt, she didn't have the time. Or the inclination. Or
her head in the right place to be able to make getting
in and out of that kind of rendezvous any simpler than
getting in and out of the gelataria was turning out to
be.

'How about, first things first, we start you off with
a real coffee?' he suggested, the cheeky slant to his all-
too-knowing smile making her stomach flip, sending
the butterflies darting for cover.

'No, thanks. This one's just fine,' Morgan insisted, lifting her cold cup between them.

'It's far from fine,' he said. 'It hasn't steamed since you walked in.'

'I don't mind cold coffee,' she said.

He raised an eyebrow. 'I do. It physically hurts me to see it. So you're getting a new one. Skinny latte, right? Double shot. No sugar.'

She opened her mouth. Shut it. Then lifted her cardboard cup to see if the coffee-shop kid had written on the side. He hadn't. 'How on earth could you possibly know that?'

'It's a talent.' He held out a hand for her half-drunk, not even half-enjoyed, coffee. After a moment's hesitation, she moved close enough to pass it to him. His fingers brushed against hers as he took her cup. For less than a split second. And it felt as if she'd been stung. She was obviously the only one to feel that way as he just smiled and tossed the cup unceremoniously into a bin below the counter.

But his quite divine dark brown eyes didn't leave hers as he plucked ingredients and implements from drawers and shelves and set about making her a new coffee. She couldn't look away. It was as if she were watching an expert juggler. If she blinked she'd miss the trick.

Okay, so asking questions was only prolonging her stay when she really ought to move along, but she had to know. 'What about me screamed skinny double-shot latte?'

'Do you really want to know?' His dark eyes darkened, his deep voice deepened. And her stomach kind of turned in on itself. 'Do you really want to know?' he asked.

'I really want to know.'

When he began to shoot steam through the jug of hot milk he finally looked away, and she felt herself slide back into her shoes, as if she had been let off some kind of hook that had been keeping her on her tiptoes.

'Rightio,' he said, pouring the double espresso shot then hot milk into a large crystal cut-glass. 'Women who look like you look always drink skim milk and avoid sugar like the plague even though guys like me secretly think you could do with a couple more kilos on your frame.'

She made a move to protest, to tell him that she had to be this size to be able to fit into the free clothes her job with the magazine afforded her, another reason she put up with Alicia and no social life, but he held up a hand to silence her.

'And the double shot part comes down to your fingernails.'

'My fingernails?' She glanced down at her basic French tips.

'They say fancy career gal or yummy mummy. Either way you're in a demographic that looks on caffeine as a major food group.'

His smile grew, deep crinkles fanning out around his warm brown eyes. Beneath the stubble and too-long hair the guy had an overabundance of confidence. Which should have been a complete turn-off. Instead all that straight-up self-assurance struck an incongruous chord somewhere deep inside her. Learning how to be that way would be a far better trick than juggling or blindfold espresso-making.

'Which is it, then?' he asked, before licking foam from the end of his long index finger.

She probably should have shot him down in flames by inventing a pro-wrestler husband and three-year-old twins, but as she watched his long finger slide through his teeth the words, 'Career girl, one hundred per cent,' shot out of her mouth.

'Scary, aren't I?' he asked.

In more ways than one, she thought. She glanced at her watch, not having anywhere else to be, but he didn't know that. And she knew a thing or two about selling an image, too. Let him focus on the fact that she was a fancy career girl. Too busy for all this chit-chat. Too fancy for him. And maybe she'd get out of here in one piece.

He ignored her hint and took the end of a spoon, etched a pattern into the white foam bringing filaments of brown coffee through and up. He wrapped a chocolate brown serviette around the glass, tucking in the side in a practised move before sliding the drink over to her.

She moved in just close enough to see into the glass to find two curly letter x's marked the foam. Her mouth twitched into a smile. 'Kiss kiss,' she said, translating the name of the shop into English.

'Right back at you,' he said.

Though the words brought forth hazy memories of the last time she had gone on a date that included a really satisfying kiss, much less a kiss kiss, she put his comment down to an occupational tic and didn't take it personally. She wasn't here to do personal. She was quite taken with the 'every girl for herself' theory, and thus far she was still alive and kicking with a well-preserved heart. She planned on leaving Melbourne the same way. And soon.

Morgan reached into her handbag for her purse, only to have Barista Boy wrap a sudden hand around her wrist. Lean fingers hung on with length to spare. Gently, but with enough pressure to stop her in her tracks as she stared at the point where their skin touched. Warmed. Zinged.

She was enveloped in the comforting scent of cinnamon. His scent. She breathed slow and deep through her nose. Had it really been that long since she'd had *satisfaction* of any kind? It must have been for her to be getting hot under the collar over a little wrist and scent action.

'Consider it a taste test,' he said, his deep voice rumbling through his arm into hers, causing tremors to slither under her skin like a river of small electrical shocks. 'Once you've had Bacio Bacio, you never go back.'

She twisted gently until he let go of her arm, his long, warm fingers sliding away, leaving her wrist tingling as though she'd hit her funny bone.

'I see through your little marketing ploy,' she said, making a great show of putting away her beaded purse as if that was why she wanted her arm back in the first place. 'Get people hooked and the initial investment will come back to you tenfold. Being on the receiving end of many such taste tests in my line of work, I promise it only works if your product is out of this world. Otherwise it's just free stuff.'

He held his hands out, palms up. 'And?'

She blinked up at him. Then at the steaming coffee and its chocolate-brown kisses. Rather than pushing her luck any further, Morgan took a polite sip. The sip turned into a mouthful. The mouthful became a good ten seconds of slow, slippery, hot, just bitter enough, rich, creamy, culinary heaven with a caffeine kick that coursed through her veins in a wave of pure grateful pleasure. This backstreet barista's latte was so far out of this world it belonged in another galaxy entirely.

Her analysis must have been pretty obvious, as he flattened both hands on the counter, leaned in towards her and drawled, 'Now don't you want to know what other talents I possess?'

Despite herself, Morgan coughed out another laugh. She risked eye contact only to kick herself mentally when the backs of her knees melted in response. Flattering though it was, it was time to put a stop to this. For all intents and purposes she held the poor guy's job in the palm of her hand. 'Not so much,' she said.

'I'd be happy to write you a list,' he said, either not noticing her deliberate retreat or ignoring it. 'Give you time to ponder it later. Tonight perhaps, when you're all alone in your room, snuggled tight under the blanket, reminiscing over every detail of our first meeting.'

'I don't need a list. You've just given away that subtle flirtation is not on there.'

'*Touché,*' he said. She laughed again. Something she hadn't expected to have spent much time doing this week. She shook her head, wondering how on earth she'd managed to become nonplussed by a grown man in a baseball cap and an apron.

She shot him a half-smile, then she and her super latte scooted down to the far end of the counter to pretend to be taken with the glistening concoctions in the glass cabinets. She realised that from the moment she'd walked inside she'd forgotten that outside it was mid-winter.

That was the fantasy whoever designed this place was trying to sell. A perennial Tuscan summer. And it worked. With this guy working the room it only grounded her growing supposition that this business at least was a raging success.

Therefore with a string of out-of-this-world retailers, and a facelift of monumental proportions, this precinct might not turn out to be the white elephant she feared it might be. It might really be…something.

She absent-mindedly took another heavenly sip to find the latte tasted even better than she remembered. She had to tighten her toes so as not to shiver in pure bliss.

The creator of said goose-bumps thankfully hadn't noticed her sadly near-orgasmic response. He was lovingly wiping down his machine with a red cloth. All fluid wrist action and avid concentration brought the brass to a high shine. She wondered if those hands were as skilled at other endeavours as they were with a dish-cloth…

She blinked furiously, then looked down into her half-drunk latte. What the hell did he put into this besides milk, hot water, and ground coffee beans?

She glanced up again as Barista Boy threw the cloth over his shoulder, then scratched under his chin, back to front, mouth turned down like some gangster in a movie. He didn't look classically Italian, though with his dark hair and those bottomless brown eyes she could make that stretch.

His eyes slid her way and she was caught staring. Staring and admiring. She quickly looked up as though taken with the moulded cornices. Well, look at that. They were spectacular. Somebody at some stage had put a lot of devotion into dressing this place. Someone who understood the selling power of warmth and comfort. And she who had never thought herself the type to need either had been drawn inexorably in.

Saxon wiped his hands on his apron and sauntered over to the gelato cabinet. Or more precisely towards the dirty blonde.

Summer or winter, people travelled miles just for a double scoop of pistachio and peppermint, a bucket of smooth vanilla, or his favourite combination of equal parts Bacio and cinnamon. He was interested to find out where her tastes lay. Sweet or sour. Creamy or textured. Layered with flavour, shot through with smooth melted chocolate, or sharp biscuit, or au naturel.

Picking someone's drink tastes was a party trick he'd picked up working nights in a bar through his university days. But a person's favourite gelato was nuanced. It had more to do with memory than lifestyle. And everything about this woman was so far a delicious mystery.

'You've never been in here before, have you?' he said.

She shook her head.

'Well, then, you can't possibly be a Melbournite.'

A smile twinkled in her somewhat wary eyes, and tickled at the corners of her naturally down-turned mouth. 'You're psychic, right? That's your *one* big talent.'

He laughed. She was funny. Prickly, but funny. Lemon and pineapple, for sure. No toppings. 'I'm thinking you have in fact left your husband and fancy career back in…Sydney.'

She laughed, but for some reason tried to hide it

behind her coffee glass. 'Wrong. No husband in Sydney, or the city in which I do live. Sorry. You lose a point.'

'Okay. But I'm close. I can feel it.'

She shrugged. Her dramatic eyes skimmed quickly to him, then back to the gelato. But she was only pretending. She was focussed one hundred per cent on him. Until she dived back into the coffee.

The moment the warm glass touched her lips her eyes fluttered closed and he could all but hear the moan of pleasure. He felt it in his gut. Her visceral reaction to his creation. Wow, if she was this moved by a hot drink, imagine how she might react to his famous carbonara. Or even better, his lemon pancakes the next morning…

'Put me out of my misery,' he begged. *In every which way. Please!* 'Even I'm beginning to believe that my talents were all nothing bar a beautiful dream. Where are you from?'

And how long are you here? What's your favourite dessert? Where do you most like to be kissed? Do your gorgeous eyes change colour when you are aroused to the point of pain? How do you like your eggs in the morning?

She took another long, slow sip of his coffee, this time watching him from over the top of the glass. He wasn't imagining it. Her breathtaking eyes were cagey. Sceptical even. But though every other part of her seemed to be carefully constructed, from her perfectly unkempt hair to her fingernails to her fancy schamncy outfit, her eyes were like an open book.

Wide open. So wide he found himself in grave danger of simply falling in. He was absolutely sure that if he missed the opportunity to get to know more about this woman than her favourite coffee blend, he would regret it more than was entirely prudent.

Just as he decided that was good enough reason to leave her well enough alone, she looked up at him from beneath her lashes. 'Paris. I'm visiting from Paris.'

He tucked his fingers over the edge of the freezer, hoping it might cool him down. 'Ah-h, Paris. The city of love,' he said. 'You can get a good coffee there, sure, but the ice cream is awful.'

She laughed, and this time didn't have the chance to cover it up. The husky sound filled the room, purring along his skin and tingling in the ends of his fingers. Fingers that he gripped tight against the cold metal so as not to lose himself in thoughts of tucking those long dishevelled waves behind her ears, leaving her face all eyes before he leaned in and tasted the woman behind the cautious smiles.

He licked dry lips. 'And what brought you here all the way from Paris?'

'Here to Melbourne, or here to this humble neck of the woods?' she asked, her eyes losing a small measure of their newfound brightness as she hid once more behind her stunning green fortress.

Saxon's skin began to itch again. In earnest. He reminded himself that, though she was pretty and pint-sized and made him want to beat his chest like Tarzan, she lived far far away, was wary and kind of skittish, and she still hadn't ordered a gelato. *She still hadn't ordered a gelato...* If that wasn't why she had come in, then what was she after?

'You choose,' he said, stretching out his fingers, crossing his arms and leaning his hip against the counter. 'You are here because...'

'My grandfather died,' she said, and her guarded gaze didn't falter. She didn't even blink. Cool little miss.

'I'm sorry,' he said. And he was. He was thirty-three and hadn't lost a grandparent yet. He had come close to losing his own father, not all that many years before. The memory created a ball as cold as ice in the centre of his gut. Family was everything to him, something that had only become more obvious after his own marriage had fallen apart.

She gave a small shrug, but he noticed that her hands shook as she finished off the coffee in one last gulp and placed the glass on the counter. She wasn't cool. She was lovely. 'I didn't know him at all,' she said. 'Still, I had to come back to take care of some of the provisions of his will.'

He nodded, though all he knew was that he knew way less about what was really going on than he thought he ought to. By this stage his toes itched. His spine itched. Even his hair itched.

'So my turn for a question,' she said.

'Go ahead.'

'What's a *talented* guy like you doing working in a place like this?' she asked, peeling the napkin from the outside of the glass.

'I own it. It's been in my family for four generations,' he said, watching as she smudged the corner of the napkin across her lips, dragging pink skin sideways, until the plump softness sprang back into shape. He was glad he was hidden from the waist down behind the counter right about then.

'Right,' she said, wincing as she shoved the screwed-up napkin into the empty glass. 'Of course it has.'

It was coming. The reason behind the itch. And this green-eyed vixen was bringing it with her all the way. 'So if you're not in fact here to taste my infamous wares, then what are you doing here, Miss…?'

'Morgan Kipling-Rossetti,' she said, holding out a slim hand.

'That's some name.'

'Blame my mother.'

'Mine named me Saxon,' he said. 'Ciantar. The blame is ongoing.' He took her hand. It was so small, so delicate, but the handshake was strong, practised, resolute. It heralded bad news. He could just feel it. Tripping and skipping up his arm from the point of contact all the way to his tight lungs like an escalating current. He let go first.

Kipling? He searched his mental databanks for where he might have met her before, because he sure knew the name.

'I'm Barton Kipling's granddaughter,' she said with a ghost of a smile. 'And I'm here, Saxon Ciantar, because he left me this building in his will. I'm your new landlord.'

And just like that Saxon's itch had a name. And its name was Morgan Kipling-Rossetti.

CHAPTER TWO

OF COURSE the sexy stranger was Saxon's new landlord. He would not have felt so strong an attraction towards her unless she was in a position to screw with him. It was the story of his damn life.

He ran a hand across his mouth, stubble grazing his palm, the sharp texture biting into his skin, helping him focus his thoughts.

Kipling had been an old-fashioned guy, a lover of aged scotch and Sinatra, both of which the two of them had indulged in every year near Christmas. But he had also been a stubborn so-and-so who had refused every offer Saxon had ever made to buy the Como Avenue strip. Now he knew why. The granddaughter waiting in the wings.

'The old man left all five shopfronts to you?' Saxon asked, biding his time while he tried to jam new pieces into the old puzzle.

'That's right.' Morgan nodded, waves of dark blonde hair falling like curtains down her cheeks, shading her luminous eyes. Eyes that watched him carefully. Not nervously, or imperiously, or with barely concealed lust, just…carefully.

He ought to tread just as carefully. This roadblock to his resolute plan for this place wasn't the usual tight-fisted suit. She was a singular small blonde who three minutes before had had him so turned on he would have given up his weekly fight with cousin Darius if that was what it would have taken to get her to agree to see him again. More. Now. Five minutes from now. Tonight. Tomorrow…

He closed his eyes for longer than a blink. The itch had been trying to tell him something. To warn him to tread lightly. He searched deep inside himself for whatever deeply hidden careful genes he might possess.

When he opened his eyes again he smiled warmly and leant his palms on the counter. The picture of the perfect host. 'Now, Morgan, lovely as it has been to meet you face to face, you didn't have to come all the way from Paris to collect the rent.'

'That's not why I am here, Saxon,' she said, all but purring his name right back at him. She smiled, and he knew that it was as artificial as his own.

His pulse began to beat hard against the back of his head as he tried to second- and third-guess her. And to ignore that small but loud part of his brain focussing instead on the rise and fall of her chest, the hint of pink warming her throat, the new adrenalin-fuelled brilliance in her eyes.

'Great,' he said, 'because we always pay the real-estate agent two doors up. I would think, considering you live so very far away from our humble street, it would be easier keeping it that way.'

'Would it now?' she asked, and her smile grew in direct proportion to the enthusiasm in her eyes, which faded to a tiny glint within her large pupils. A fierce, tenacious glint that made the blood rush harder and hotter through his veins.

Think, he demanded of himself. *Focus and think.*

She was here for some reason. Perhaps she had known who he was all along and was awaiting the right moment to make her move. To let him know she might go where her grandfather had not and sell him the land beneath his feet. Perhaps this little *femme fatale* was in fact the answer to all his dreams.

Images of roaring fires, shag-pile rugs at Mt Buller clouded his thoughts again, though this time the girl accompanying him had a face.

He needed to let *her* think she was in charge. She was her grandfather's granddaughter after all. 'Unless…' he said, letting the word hang on the air between them like a pretty promise.

'Unless?' she repeated like a good girl.

The brass bell over the front door tinkled and a group of teenaged girls came bustling inside. They stared at Saxon, stopped talking, then started giggling in earnest before hustling over to the gelato. He'd run out of time. And he couldn't let her go until he knew more. Until he knew everything. 'How about we discuss this in further detail over steak, soufflé and a bottle of Sav Blanc sound?'

She gave one long stunned blink, then her right hand fluttered to her chest. 'You're asking me out to dinner?'

'That I am,' he said, wondering why he hadn't simply asked before. If he'd known he would receive this delectable wide-eyed response he would have asked the moment he'd thought of it, which was the second she'd walked through his door. Which was why he followed up with the brilliant, 'Unless you'd prefer Perry Como, a bottle of red and pizza on my lounge-room floor?'

She gaped at him as though he had suddenly started speaking Swahili. He didn't blame her. He'd had no idea those words were coming until he'd said them. His libido had taken one last leap of faith, tripped over its own ego and fallen flat on its face.

'You can't blame a guy for trying, right?' He smiled quickly, broadly, to prove that he had of course been kidding around.

She smiled thinly, then scrounged around her large bag until she came up with a card and a pen. He bent forward to see the card read 'Morgan Kipling-Rossetti, *Chic* Magazine, Paris'. She turned the card over, lay it flat on the counter, bent from the hip, and in flourishing script wrote her hotel name and room number on the back.

Her gold sweater tipped forward until he had a bird's-eye view of a pink lace bra and the swell of some rather lovely cleavage. She was so close he could see that her hair was a rainbow concoction of carefully painted levels of blonde. It likely took her three hours a month to keep it looking that way. But she was also so close her perfume drifted to him, hot, piquant, like black cherries. God, but she was tempting. Surely two mature people with their eyes wide open could mix business and pleasure without causing any irreparable damage.

Then again perfume like that was more expensive per ounce than gold. And women like her were all-consuming. And he wasn't in the market to be that guy. Never again. His priority was with the business. The family.

Yep. He was glad he had that sorted.

Once she was done writing she stood and he found himself face to face. She had a small dark mole, the size

of a pen mark just below her right eye. It was so sexy
he gripped the counter.

She passed him her card. 'Call me later,' she said. 'I
think there is enough for us to discuss that would warrant
steak. But I'd prefer the red wine if that's still on offer.'

Her mouth curved into a sexy half-smile, before it
disappeared inside an uneasy frown. And then she, her
wary green eyes, her petite curves and the itch she
brought with her turned and mercifully walked out his
front door before he did anything else he'd later be
forced to beat himself up over.

Saxon spent the afternoon chasing up the other retailers in the Como Avenue strip. It turned out Morgan had
already done the rounds. And though none of them
could quite pinpoint what about her had made them
nervous, they had all felt it too.

Cassie and Lenny Chang of the dry-cleaner's thought
it was the fact that her handbag was so very large.
Morris and Adele Cosgrove, the real-estate agents, said
she paced their establishment like a caged cat. Ignatius
and Sangeeta Puran of the Indian restaurant had offered
her a free butter chicken, their house speciality, but she
had claimed she wasn't hungry. Nobody was ever too
full for a Punjabi Palace butter chicken.

Only Jan Sager had openly liked her. Apparently
Morgan had spent an hour perusing her mishmash of
haberdashery, buying fabric samples, taking a whole
box of odd buttons, and at one point even going so far
as to call her shop a 'smorgasbord of delights'.

Once Saxon was over the fact that he'd barely been
able to convince her to sample a coffee, and that Jan and
her crazy beads had outdistanced him and his gelato by

a good forty minutes, he focussed on the more salient
fact that Jan thought her a sensible and sympathetic
woman who would do the right thing if left to her own
devices. Though he was fairly sure there was more than
just herbs in the tea Jan drank like water.

Later, sitting in the lounge room of his large open-
plan beachside Brighton home, he pulled the sleek
white business card from the back pocket of his jeans,
and fingered the corner. No matter which way he
decided to play it, Morgan Kipling-Rossetti was a
woman he had no intention of leaving to her own
devices.

He dialled her hotel room. After a dozen rings he was
ready to hang up when a female voice came on the
phone. 'Hello?'

The sleepy languor trickled warmly down his spine.
'Morgan, it's Saxon Ciantar.'

Her silent pause spoke volumes. It seemed he hadn't
been quite as close to the front of her mind as she had
been to his. With a wry smile he added, 'From Bacio
Bacio Gelataria. On Como Avenue.'

'I know,' she said, her voice slow and smooth as hot
treacle. 'I was just yawning.'

'You were asleep?'

'*Oui*,' she said on a sigh. A soft, lethargic, warm,
sexy French sigh that had Saxon thinking of mounds of
pillows, tangled white cotton sheets wrapped around her
glorious female limbs. 'I only got into Melbourne this
morning and I don't cope with flying all that well.
Flying, change of latitude, lack of sleep, customs, cabs
driving on the wrong side of the road, walking upside
down on the bottom of the world. I'm awake now, so
what can I do for you?'

'Dinner. Tonight,' he said, feeling as if he were sixteen again and trying to act cool, and experienced, while his voice croaked as badly as it had when he'd first asked out Maryanne Putney, the love of his life. Maryanne had accepted, they'd dated, and she'd broken his heart when she'd kissed his best friend.

Later down the track he'd met another girl he'd thought to be the love of his life. Adriana, a good Italian girl. That one he'd even gone so far as to marry. She had broken his family and his business on her path of destruction as well as his heart.

Now several years on, older, and a little wiser, he was no longer in the market for the love of his life. Or anything close. He didn't trust his instincts on that score one iota. Twice bitten and all that. He did love women: their soft curves, their hidden desires and the moment he saw in their eyes that they would be his. That was more than enough. For now and for ever. Amen.

So what was so special about this woman that she had him feeling like a cat on a hot tin roof?

'Right. Yes, of course,' Morgan said several moments later, and his contrary subconscious was newly bombarded with images of her slipping out of all that tangled cotton, naked bar remnants of black cherry perfume, and slowly sliding a satin robe over her slim shoulders. 'So where shall I meet you?'

He momentarily considered giving her his home address instead. It would take nothing for him to whip up a quick pasta. They could eat on his secluded deck, captive to the magnificent view of an early sunset over Port Phillip Bay, and see where the night took them.

He had to clear his throat to dislodge the hazy desire thickening his windpipe. Tonight things were already in motion to make that not an option. 'How about you meet me in the bar off the foyer of your hotel at say eight, and we can go from there?'

'Eight. Hotel bar,' she repeated. 'Fine.'

'Until then,' he said, and hung up, placing the phone onto his glass-topped coffee-table before running both hands over his face.

Until then he had forces to marshal, avenues to block and possibilities to map out. Her initial arrival had been a surprise attack. The next time he met with Morgan Kipling-Rossetti, he would be fully prepared.

The trip to Melbourne had been last-minute, therefore Morgan had packed quickly and ended up with too many shoes, enough costume jewellery to drown a cat, barely enough underwear and mostly trans-seasonal clothes as she hated the cold and never remembered how bad winter could be until she was in the middle of it.

The only going-out clothing she had was a sparkly green Versace dress she'd snaffled from Alicia's left-overs after the previous month's fashion shoots. Backless it was, with a split up the thigh, feathered layers heavy with crystals, and a spaghetti strap on one shoulder leaving the other bare.

It was no doubt far too sexy for a business-meeting-slash-date-slash-who-knew-what, but it fitted her like a glove. The colour set off her eyes like nothing else and the cut made the most of her faint summer tan, which would fade the instant she returned home to an insanely heavy workload to make up for this time away.

She squared her shoulders in the mirror and con-vinced herself the dress was less an outfit and more a costume. That was the thing that had attracted her to fashion in the first place: the ability to become whoever you wanted to be simply by choosing a skirt over pants, a red lipstick over pink, big sunglasses over none.

A dress like this wasn't just a dress—it was body armour. And she'd need as much confidence as she could get to come up against the likes of Saxon Ciantar again.

She needed the flirting to stop, and the peculiar tummy tingles to go away. Because she was here to get in and get out and to do that she needed him on board. The way the other Como Avenue retailers had deferred to him constantly hit that home. And she needed it to happen as soon as possible.

Her boss had left a frantic message on her cell phone as she'd slept. Every second she was here her work was falling behind. Photographic schedules were collapsing in on one another. Panic! Panic! When would she be back?

Soon, she hoped. Before other set designers took up enough of the slack and Alicia realised she was replaceable. In her experience loyalty always came a poor second to assurance. At work. In relationships. It was that whole 'every girl for herself' thing all over again.

At five to eight she added oversized gold hoops, and tiny diamond studs that had been a gift from her father for her sixteenth birthday, grabbed her sparkly clutch purse, tugged on a pair of nude two-inch-heeled sandals, and headed out the door.

At the hotel bar she ordered a dirty martini, and waited with her back to the room for Saxon to find her. She and her *über*-dress needed to sell the image of a cool, sophisticated, busy career gal with time only for business. Not funny business. If she actually pulled it off she might never take the dress off ever again.

She was barely halfway through her drink when she felt a presence move in behind her. It was him. She knew by the wall of male warmth shifting against her naked back creating swirls of reverberating heat through her chest, by the scent of cinnamon wafting past her willing nostrils, and by the look of wide-eyed admiration on the face of the female bartender.

She then took a moment to finish her drink, twirled the toothpick between her fingers and turned with the gin-soaked olive caught between her teeth.

When she saw that Saxon was not alone, that he was in fact surrounded by all seven other retailers of Como Avenue, she got such a jolt of surprise she swallowed the olive whole. Not all the way, of course. It got neatly jammed in just the right spot to cut off her air supply.

Right about the time tears began pouring from her eyes, Saxon asked, 'Hey, are you all right?'

She held up a finger, while her other fist thumped against her chest.

The others stood back and watched her with a mix of self-righteousness and fascination. Saxon ignored her eloquent finger, and moved in, placed a hand around her waist to twist her on her chair before giving her one great thump on the back.

Whether it was the hit, pure embarrassment, or the electric jolt of his touch on her naked skin, it worked. Her breathing returned to normal.

A white napkin appeared in her eye line; she took it to wipe beneath her eyes and gave Saxon a short, furious smile in thanks. And while she wanted to crawl over the bar and hide on the other side, he smiled back, all crinkling dark eyes and charm and pure, unadulterated sex appeal.

He'd shaved, his hair was slicked back off his face, and he wore a dashing charcoal dark suit with a pistachio-green open-necked shirt. And while half of her still wanted to thump him right on back the other half—the reactive half, the half she preferred to keep tamed and under wraps lest it make her say and do things she would later regret—wanted to grab him by the collar and pull him over the other side of the bar with her.

She quite sensibly did neither. From here on she would be the model of Parisienne sophistication and ennui, not a woman struggling to come to terms with being home, alone, and unwittingly embroiled in family politics she'd thought she'd left behind a decade before when her reactive side had taken over and sent her screaming from her mother's house and the only city she'd ever known and she'd not looked back…

'I see you've brought some friends along,' she said, when she'd found her voice. 'How thoughtful.'

'You've met already,' he said. 'So there is no need to introduce you all.'

'No need. So nice to see you all again, and so soon.' She spun all the way around on her chair and smiled. She received a couple of smiles in return, and a couple of frowns. While Morris Cosgrove, one half of the brother-and-sister act who ran the real-estate agency, was finding the split in the side of her dress fascinating.

She wanted to heave the fabric over her exposed leg, but when she saw that Saxon's gaze had landed there as well she realised that more than anything she wanted to put her hands around his neck and squeeze.

Sophistication? Ennui? Bah! She was wearing Versace for *him*. She'd washed her hair for *him*. She'd put on lip-gloss and dabbed perfume in dips and crevices all over her body for him. And not just to get him on her side. But in some out-of-character, purely female hope that the last thing he had wanted to do with her that night was talk business.

And whether he was psychic, or just experienced enough to know when a woman found him undeniably attractive, Saxon knew it.

'Shall we move to a more convenient setting?' he asked. 'Perhaps the couches in the centre of the bar would suit.'

She swallowed, reminding herself he meant they would be more suitable for a round-table chat, not…other pursuits. *French sophistication*, she reminded herself. *Ennui*. On a daily basis she dealt with histrionic designers, touchy advertising execs, off-the-wall taxi drivers, randy bisexual designers, and her boss, Neurotic Alicia. She could deal with one rakish gelato-shop owner and his motley hangers on. 'That sounds just fine,' she said, managing a tolerant smile.

He held out a hand to help her down off the high stool. She took it—feeling like a lady alighting from a horse-drawn carriage, while also feeling like a half-dozen people were hoping she might fall flat on her face.

His hand slipped out of hers then snuck around her waist to rest at the juncture between fabric and skin at her lower back as he pressed her in the direction he wanted to go. Her skin heated and contracted at his touch and she desperately hoped he couldn't feel it too.

If they hadn't had an audience she would not have hesitated to reach back, grab that meandering little hand

and bend it so far backward the guy would be on his knees in three seconds flat.

'I apologise,' he said, so close her hair tickled against her right ear and the sleeve of his jacket brushed lengthways down her back.

'For anything in particular?' she asked, angry at him, but more angry at herself for being blinded by a little harmless flirtation and not seeing any of this coming. 'Or can I take my pick?'

His hand moved higher so that his fingers could strum her spine as if it were a harp. 'When I hit you on the back trying to save your life I left a red mark.'

'You didn't save my life, Saxon. You merely saw a chance to humble me.' She twisted to look over her shoulder but couldn't see a thing. 'I just might sue.'

When she faced the front, he splayed his long fingers over the spot. His palm rested hot and firm against her sensitive skin. A voluptuous shiver threatened but she caught it in time. As a suit of armour so far her damn dress was leaving a lot to be desired. No wonder in the olden days they went for neck-to-toe steel.

'It'll fade before you have the chance to prove a thing,' he said.

'Here's hoping,' she said beneath her breath. If the memory of his every touch didn't fade she wasn't sure her current concentration levels could stretch beyond it. 'It didn't occur to you to warn me that I might need to book a larger table?'

'Forewarned is forearmed, they say.'

She glanced sideways. Bad idea. For he had some profile. A strong nose, deep-set dark eyes, and a mouth so perfectly carved and sensuous her own lips tingled. She scraped her teeth over them to wipe the sensation away.

'If I'd known this was going to be an intervention I would have hired a room. Maybe even a soapbox just for you.'

The hollow beneath his cheekbone grew deep and dark as his mouth creased into a humourless smile. 'This is no intervention, Morgan. This is a fight to the death.'

'We are at war? I had no idea.'

'Consider yourself told.' He glanced at her, and the intensity in his eyes made her lose her footing. For the briefest of moments. But he noticed. He noticed and he smiled. He smiled and her stomach turned to molten lava.

He dropped his hand, but not before letting his warm fingers trail across her skin one last time. Slow, deliberate, as though this time when he left his mark upon her he meant it.

'Ladies,' Saxon called out, sweeping an arm towards a set of long deep sofas and matching high-backed chairs in the centre of the room.

As they took their seats Cassie Chang clutched her handbag to her chest as though she thought Morgan might leap over the table and steal it. *Smart woman,* Morgan thought. For there was a good chance she was about to take more from Cassie than the meagre contents of her purse.

She leant back in a solo chair, crossed her legs and wished that she'd just bitten the bullet and forked out for a property lawyer to deal with them on her behalf. But apart from not being able to afford it, her mother's second husband Julian was a top property lawyer himself, or he had been nine-odd years ago when Pamela had up and married him practically before Morgan's dad had been cold in the ground. If property law was as gossipy and incestuous as fashion was, her mother would find out she was here in the blink of an eye.

She looked at the anxious faces across from her and fought to swallow the overwhelming decade-old resentment towards her mother, and lifetime resentment towards her grandfather. This conversation was going to be hard enough as it was.

'We may as well get to the point,' she said. Her gaze landed upon Saxon. He sat directly opposite her, as if he had chosen that position so she could feel his persuasive eyes upon her the whole time. Then she motioned to her dress and said, 'I have dinner plans. So the sooner we get through this, the better.'

Saxon's mouth slid effortlessly into a sexy smile. A teasing warmth spread through her abdomen like a red wine stain on white linen. Unfortunately that was the kind of thing that always left a permanent mark.

'Fine,' he said, his deep voice flowing across the air to caress her bare skin. She wondered if any of the other women in the group could feel it too or whether his talents extended to focussing the effects with pinpoint accuracy. Then he said, 'I asked you here tonight to try to convince you to sell.'

Her stunned glance swung from him to the other now-eager faces. So *that* was what this summit was all about? She felt a wave of disappointment on their behalf. And, truth be told, on hers. For that would have solved all their problems in one fell swoop.

'I'm afraid I can't do that,' she said, casting apologetic glances at each of the shop owners. But they weren't in the market for an apology. 'Have you ever thought of moving? To a more inviting location. A city hub, perhaps, or a successful suburban shopping centre. Surely—'

'The Como Avenue precinct has been as it is for decades,' real-estate agent Adele Cosgrove said. 'We all have family-owned businesses. Businesses we have built so that they support our families. Our children.'

'Our grandchildren,' Cassie Chang added, clutching tighter to her purse as though Morgan might now be after the wallet-sized photos therein.

'Managing a real-estate portfolio is a tough job,' Saxon continued, unabated. It seemed he wasn't the kind of guy to take no for an answer. 'It involves knowledge of councils and inflation and contract law. Surely not the kind of thing a busy jet-setting career gal like you would be interested in.'

His gaze flicked to her 'career gal' fingernails, which meant she had to cease wringing her hands. She crossed her arms instead. But it only drew his gaze to her naked *décolletage*. It then took its time moving back to her eyes by way of her bare shoulders, her lips, her warming cheeks. He added, 'I would truly be more than happy to take the lot off your hands for a compensatory price.'

He shot her a verbal offer. Off the cuff. Without blinking. Without demurring. In the millions. At that her cool fell apart. Her mouth literally dropped open and she began to blink as if she had walked into a blizzard.

With that kind of financial injection a person could tell the dictator in heels to shove her tacky Bahamas and banana-daiquiri-favoured layouts. Morgan could buy an apartment in a nicer part of Paris, even one with heating. She wouldn't need to rely on free clothes to keep her head above water monetarily. But more importantly she could pick and choose jobs that truly stretched her and moved her; shabby chic and renaissance vogue, film sets and private homes, all dripping in her beloved bohemian ideals of beauty, truth, and freedom. And love. The easy love of architecture, sunsets, cashmere, ridiculously expensive shoes; the kinds of things she could never make the mistake of expecting to love her back.

Saxon must have picked up on her delirium, for she could sense him mentally punching the air. A couple of heads in her peripheral vision nodded profusely. And her dangerous flight of fancy came to a thudding halt.

'Sell it to me, Morgan,' Saxon said, his deep voice calling to her from the other side of the low coffee-table.

Me? Not us. Where on earth was he getting his hands on such funds? Tips? Spare change from the back pocket of his jeans? A kissing booth at the Melbourne show? That last one she found herself half believing.

Morgan licked her lips and looked away, deciding that Morris Cosgrove with his suggestive leer was actually a better option for her focus than Saxon's anything. 'I thought I made myself clear. I *can't* sell.'

'Can't schman't,' Saxon said, and her eyes shot back to his as if she were a puppet on his string. 'All it takes is one little signature on one little bit of paper and you make a load of money. Then we can move on and let the fun part begin. Champagne. Streamers. And what-ever else the night may bring us.'

The others took up the catch cry, leaning forward and telling her why it would be so good for her to let Saxon buy the decrepit old building. How nice it would be for them all if she just went home.

To Paris. Where she worked with people who would

never come to her defence like these people had for one another at the drop of a hat. She shook her head. That had never mattered to her before. In fact she kind of preferred things that way. Disconnected. Not messing with anyone else's business, and nobody messing with hers. She could go on scouting out mini umbrellas and brightly coloured food dye for fake daiquiris for a living to keep that kind of sanctuary.

'No, I *can't* sell to you,' she said, this time more forcibly. And everyone shut up so quickly her words hung heavily on the air. 'It was a provision of my grandfather's will. I am not allowed to sell. Even if I want to. Not for nine years.' The exact same amount of time since she had spoken to her mother. Barton's daughter. It was no coincidence, she was sure.

'And if I decide to sell at that time,' she continued, her voice getting faster and higher as she delivered the killer blow, 'I have a contract, signed before Barton died, giving first right of refusal to a local developer.'

Saxon's face lost colour. His drop in composure impressed upon her deeply. He was cocky. A hotshot. Pure confidence. Well, of course he was. That was why she had agreed to meet with him. In Versace. With clean, styled hair. But she'd genuinely pained him. She who'd trodden softly through life, alone, specifically so as not to cause pain to anybody. For she knew exactly what it felt like to be on the receiving end. Her chair felt as if it were tipping sideways. Her heart rate doubled. And she began to feel hot all over.

'Right,' Saxon said, his colour returning to normal so fast she hoped it had only been a trick of the light. 'That rules out that option. So I guess my next question is: what are your plans in the interim? Will you keep the current fee structure in place? Paid through the Cosgroves?'

She glanced at Adele, who had lost far more colour than Saxon, while Morris had turned a terrible shade of purple. She wondered how much he made on the rent each month. Enough, by the sweat pouring down his brow.

She wished she could tell them all she'd never wanted any of this in the first place. That she hadn't asked to be in a position where she might be about to put people out of business. Would that she was never born a Kipling…

But, she had them all there, and she took a deep breath and pulled the bandage off in one quick rip.

'Actually, I am currently leaning toward knocking the whole building down and starting afresh. A new look. A new kind of clientele. And all new retailers. None of you have current leases. I checked. Plans have been drawn up, permits approved. It could begin as soon as a month from now.'

She expected some kind of gasp, perhaps even a wail and some beating of chests, but she was met with stony silence. She found she couldn't look at anyone but Saxon. He wasn't just the leader of the little group, he was the muscle, the backbone, and the strong one.

'You are leaning…' he said. 'Meaning you haven't yet made up your mind.'

'Well, no,' she faltered. 'I have yet to meet with the developers, their investors and the architects who Barton contracted. Nothing has been set in stone.'

'Good. That gives us time to present our case. How long are you in town?'

Too long, already, she thought, thinking of Alicia's three-second attention span. 'A week at the most. But I don't really—'

Saxon stood, and the others followed suit. 'Then give us five days. I think that's a fair request.'

'Fair?' she repeated. Was it fair that she was caught in a position where others' needs outweighed her own? That it seemed to be a recurring theme of her life. One of these days she would hit a point where all that bottled-up desire to be number one in somebody's life, even her own, would be nice, would rise to the top, spill over and create one hell of a mess.

But not tonight. Not with all of these kind-looking people frowning down at her. So scared. So rattled. Not in front of too cool Saxon. And not in Versace.

She sighed. 'Fine. You have until the weekend. If you can show me in that time why it is in *my* best interests to keep things running as they are, then I'll consider it.'

The Changs shook her hand and bowed and thanked her a hundred times. 'No promises,' she said.

The Purans patted her on the hand and thanked her from their children, and their children's children. 'Be prepared otherwise,' she said.

The Cosgroves glared and simpered by turns and she had no clue what to say to either of them. But she couldn't help but smile back when Jan Sager of the wool and fabric shop winked at her, as though she knew she would do the right thing in the end. But the right thing by whom?

When they were all gone she buried her face in her palms and kicked herself for coming back to Melbourne at all. There were too many unlaid ghosts with new ones springing up everywhere she looked. She kicked herself for agreeing to let the Como Avenue gang have a go, and trying to do the right thing. And for not being the strong, self-sufficient, stony-hearted island unto herself she so wished she could be.

'Still up for a steak?' A deep male voice washed over her naked back like warm honey.

Morgan opened her eyes and looked through her fingers at her bare knees. The longest day of her life wasn't over yet.

Saxon was back.

CHAPTER THREE

MORGAN glanced over her shoulder to find Saxon standing behind her, his hand curled over the back of her chair. He was smiling down at her as though none of the past twenty minutes had happened. As though with his dark suit and sexy smile he were a gorgeous stranger here to pick her up to take her on a date. It took some kind of convincing to remind herself that was *not* the case.

'Are you out of your mind?' she asked, every ounce of displeasure evident in her voice. So much so that a waiter who had been about to ask her if she wanted a drink, or a table, or his phone number spun on the spot and headed in the opposite direction. 'After you ambushed me? You have some kind of nerve.'

'That was unscrupulous of me, I admit,' he said. 'But Bacio Bacio is very important to me, as are the families of Como Avenue, and I wanted you to know that before you made any rash decisions.'

'What makes you think I'm ever rash?'

'Do you really want to know?' he asked, and after the last time he had read her so easily she shook her head.

He laughed. 'Despite a rather irascible side to your

personality that leaves me pretty much hot and bothered, my loyalties lie with the devils I know.'

She made him hot and bothered? The look in his eyes certainly seemed to press that message home. She tilted her chin, more to catch her breath than out of any kind of haughtiness. Still it made him grin.

'Oh, good for you and your grand principles,' she said. 'Now why don't you and your loyalties shove off and leave me alone?'

His finger uncurled from the chair back and pointed her way, reaching out but not touching her. Not quite. 'Is that what you really want?'

She glared at him, her gaze withering. But he didn't even flinch. The guy needed to be knocked down a peg or two. Or three. Until he was flat on his back with no hint of the sanctimonious smile that was currently lighting his gorgeous face.

'It would be such a waste not to take that unbelievable dress of yours out for a spin.' He said *dress*, but his gaze dropped to linger on her neck, her wrist, her left ankle. She'd almost forgotten this was what she had been secretly believing might come of her evening.

'What?' she said, her voice give-away husky. 'This old thing?'

His smile broadened. He knew the effect he had on her. She grew her own matching frown for the same reason.

He dragged his eyes away from her only long enough to snag the attention of another passing waiter. 'Table for two?'

Then he held out a hand and she had the choice to either be petulant and cause a scene, or to take it. She took it. He tucked her hand into the crook of his arm and placed his hand gently over the top as they followed the waiter. And she felt like a character in an Audrey Hepburn movie.

She looked down at where their hands touched. His was large, the knuckles strong, the fingers long, a couple of burn marks marred their sculpted male beauty. She imagined it happening at the espresso machine. She wondered who or what had captured his attention for so long that he *hadn't* been able to look away. She felt a sharp kick of envy. She looked away before she gave into the desire to run her fingers over those scars to make them all better.

The waiter led them into the restaurant proper where chandeliers in the high ceiling sent shards of warm light over the room, which by the time they hit the tables turned to muted gold.

Saxon requested a small, intimate table by the window. Through the smoked-glass fairy lights glittered from bare elm trees bordering the Melbourne city street three floors below. Shopfronts were lit bright despite the late hour. Couples, singles, groups, and tourists promenaded the long avenue in their night-time best and snuggled together to ward off the chill. But she was warm. In the beautiful hotel. In the beautiful dress she hoped made her seem far more sophisticated than she really was.

'I hope you're hungry,' her beautiful company asked.

'Starving,' she said.

Saxon smiled, and the butterflies awoke to play acrobatics beneath her skin. She pinched her thigh to bring herself back to reality. He had told her flat out that they were at war. His smile didn't mean what it felt as if it meant. He was only here to make his own stealthy reconnaissance. She would do right by herself not to forget that.

'Wine?' he asked.

God, yes! 'Red,' she said, 'thanks.'

He put in the order, then said, 'Now, don't tell me you are really considering kicking us all out on our ears.'

'Fine. I won't tell you that.'

The smile didn't budge, but his eyes contracted. This guy was a far cry from the scruffy charmer she'd agreed to have dinner with in the first place. She had the unsettling sensation that *this* guy, this paragon of *savoir-faire*, could play her like a fiddle. At the moment he was only toying with the idea. Toying with her.

'Who *are* you?' she asked.

He laughed, a deep rumbling sound that turned a dozen female heads his way. Brunettes stared, blondes glared, and a redhead over at the bar shot daggers with her eyes. Morgan would have traded places with any of them.

Let them deal with the assault on her nerves every time the guy looked her way. The river of heat coursing through her centre every time they touched. And, yes, even the torrid dreams that had swamped her the minute her head had hit the pillow that afternoon. All glowing skin, taut muscles, savvy hands, and talented lips bringing her to the brink over and over until she'd woken in a tangle of sweaty sheets to the sound of his voice on the other end of the phone and thought herself still dreaming.

Heck, she would have given them the damn building, if only dear old granddad hadn't covered that eventuality in his will as well.

'It wasn't a rhetorical question, Saxon. I've been truthful with you from the very beginning. It would seem gentlemanly if you let me know exactly what I'm up against.'

He leant forward until his arms were resting on the table, his strong hands sliding gently around one another. He flicked his hair back off his face. His dark eyes were lit gold by the dim, squat candle on their table. A stream of female sighs echoed across the room.

'Now, Morgan, what gave you the impression that I'm any kind of gentleman?'

Her butterflies developed a case of butterflies. 'Desperate hope?' she said.

He laughed again. Then leant back in his chair and squinted at her. She wished the twenty-foot window beside her could open to let in some of the freezing air outside.

'Bacio Bacio,' he finally said, 'has been in my family for four generations, beginning with the Como Avenue store when my great-grandfather came over from Italy. Over the past few years we have evolved. There are now sixty stores across Australia and New Zealand and we are about to open in London and New York in the upcoming fall. However, the Como Avenue store is the heart of the business. The heart of my family. And I will not see it fall.'

Right. Well, she had asked.

'I've shown you mine,' he said, 'now you show me yours.'

'My…'

'Cards,' he said, his lips curving into a slow, sexy smile. 'And I will believe every word you say since you have so kindly worn a dress which has no sleeves up which to hide any secret aces.' His dark gaze travelled over her bare arms, leaving a trail of warmth in its wake.

Boy, oh, boy, oh, boy.

Morgan shook off the bombardment of sensations blinding her to what was really happening. The guy might have had overt sexual energy coursing through his veins, but, apart from that one *hot and bothered* comment, he hadn't said or done anything that couldn't be seen as all business.

'Como Avenue isn't making any money,' she countered. 'What with upkeep and repairs and rising council rates it's barely in the black. It needs new plumbing, new wiring, and a new roof. And I don't know about you but I don't have extra bank accounts lying around lush with cash with which to plump up a fun little investment. If I don't find a way for this to make even the smallest profit, it would send me bankrupt.'

Saxon didn't say a word. He leant his left elbow on the table and ran his hand over his chin. As though he was trying to put himself in her shoes. She wished him luck with that. She doubted he'd ever been as broke as she had been when she'd first moved to Paris. She doubted he'd ever had to make decisions on his own as she had every day since. Come to think of it, she doubted he'd even ever doubted.

But at least he was listening. Every date she'd ever been on the guy across the table had been more interested in the sound of his own voice than in anything she had to say. She hadn't known they actually made men like Saxon any more. Maybe the big difference was that this *wasn't* a date.

'Well, then, Ms Kipling-Rossetti,' he said, his voice as low and intimate and purposeful as a caress as he picked up the bottle of wine and poured. 'It seems that you and I are at an impasse.'

'So it would seem.' Morgan deflated. Feet back to being stapled to the ground, head yanked out of the clouds. Talk about not fair.

She stared at her wineglass as Saxon filled it. She didn't say when, she just let him keep pouring until the glass was half full, and then some.

Saxon watched Morgan's shoulders slowly slump as he spun the bottle to clear up any random drips. She picked up the large glass, her small fingers clamping onto the stem, her face almost lost behind it as she took a long, deep sip.

He felt the desire to give in wash over her. If he was another kind of man he might have enjoyed the sharp taste of victory. But he was far too much of a nice guy to ever be that cutthroat. Luckily he never wanted to take over the world, just to keep his piece of it thriving.

Even if it meant sending this woman bankrupt? Even if it meant being the cause of those creases in her sweet forehead? The droop to her lovely lips? And the reason the fire within her faded and the world lost touch with something lovely?

He poured himself a glass of red and reminded himself the distraction of a woman had caused *him* to make bad decisions before. A woman who'd never once condescended to eat pizza on their lounge-room floor, instead preferring the finer things in life his money had been able to afford her. A woman who had actually been meant to be on his side, though it had turned out she'd been on nobody's side but her own.

There was a similar enough kind of fierce independence about Morgan Kipling-Rossetti that meant that no amount of wide, beseeching eyes, soft pink cheeks or crushed looks would sway him. He couldn't let them. But that didn't mean that he wouldn't do everything in his power to sway her.

He took a sip of wine and watched her pretend to pay close attention to the menu. These days he didn't need a Monaro or a newfangled hi-fi system in his car to get what he wanted. These days his particular talents lay more with his persuasive tongue.

'So tell me about Paris,' he said.

She glanced up from the menu, her wide green eyes immediately tempting him to just dive right into some full-blown affair, damn the consequences. He pressed his thumb into the palm of his hand, hard, and reminded himself they were on opposite sides of a great divide. Several great divides actually. Philosophical. Geographical. Financial.

She blinked. 'What about it?'

'Oh, I don't know. How about we start with what you do and why you do it there and not here, in the best city on earth?'

She let the menu drop, though her fingers kept a tight hold. 'I'm chief set designer for photo shoots at the French version of *Chic* Magazine. I design the layouts, buy the props, dress the sets. Like a beauty consultant for inanimate objects. And I do it there because that's where I live.' She shot him a tight smile, then plunged back into her menu.

He watched her for a few quiet seconds. 'You're a contrary woman, you know that? It would pay to be more friendly, use more honey than vinegar, to get what you desire.'

He let the last word slide from his tongue. Simply to

see what would happen. And something happened all right. Her eyes grew dark and smoky. Her cheeks pinked. She took a deep breath and let it out long and slow through her nose. And every single muscle inside his body twitched as one. He gave up pressing his thumb into his palm. What was the point? His body reacted to her in ways far further-reaching than itchy skin.

Eventually she released her white-knuckle grip on the menu and through gritted teeth she said, 'I work in Paris as the opportunities there far outweigh anywhere else when it comes to my line of work. *Haute couture* and *prêt-à-porter* are French terms after all. There. Happy?'

'Ecstatic.'

He took a sip of his drink. It was obvious she was only trying to keep him at arm's length. Which was smart, really. But then why had she had to go and wear *that* dress? It sparkled, catching the light with every tiny movement. It slid against her skin as she breathed. And it clung to her so precariously it gave the impression that all he had to do was find the exact right sequin to press and it would simply disappear in a pool of shimmering light at her feet.

He shifted in his seat, wishing he'd insisted on a different table. A longer tablecloth. A more intimate setting. Pizza, on his lounge-room floor…

The waiter returned and took their orders. He chose rare steak, the sooner it was cooked and eaten, the better. She chose marinara. It seemed they couldn't even agree on a dinner choice. She was too perverse. But then again, he was wilful and pigheaded, so they likely deserved one another.

'You are from Melbourne originally, I take it,' he said.

She nodded, and sat on her hands now that she had lost her ready-made shield in the form of the menu.

'How long have you been there?'

'Nine years.'

'You must have been a kid when you left!'

'I was seventeen.'

'Your family are over there too, then?'

She licked her bottom lip, her eyes narrowing, and he watched the wheels and cogs turn behind them as she considered his question. 'No. I moved there by myself.'

'Why Paris?'

'My father was born there. He talked of it all the time with such passion. It was never a question of whether but of when.'

'He never took you?'

She shook her head. Then shrugged. Then shook her head again. 'He passed away before he had the chance.'

'I'm sorry to hear that. He is the Rossetti part of your name, I take it?' he asked, this time more gently, more aware of the minefield he had inadvertently walked into.

She nodded again, but there was no light in her eyes. A multitude of intense warning signs, for sure. But no light. He missed the light. He wanted it back. So he took a quick conversational swerve left. 'It didn't occur to you to do the child of an ex-pat thing and just visit? Get an eyeful of the Mona Lisa, spend a year's wages on the Champs-Elysées and try a real croissant before coming back home?'

'Melbourne has its attractions,' she admitted, her pupils dilating as her eyes locked with his. Just a fraction. But that was all it took for his pulse to begin to race. 'But throw in the Eiffel Tower and Paris wins hands down.'

'Nah,' he drawled. 'This city is the best. My ancestors and others brought over the best of European culture while we still enjoy the Australian weather and sensibility. And, I see your Eiffel Tower and raise you the Melbourne Cricket Ground.'

She laughed, well, scoffed really, but there was a glimmer in her eyes, a flicker of green lightning that shot across her pupils. And suddenly he could barely keep still. His foot tapped against the carpet, and his fingers rapped a tattoo on his knee.

A stray curl hung down her cheek, and he had to ball his fist atop the table to stop from leaning over and brushing it from her face. Letting his hand linger. Running his thumb across her cheekbone.

'The MCG,' she repeated, deadpan. 'You are actually suggesting that the MCG is a reason for someone to choose Melbourne over Paris?'

Not someone, he thought. *You*. Dammit! Okay, so he wanted to touch her. And kiss her. Everywhere. It was natural. He was a man. She was a lovely, though slightly nettlesome, woman. This manifest attraction didn't mean he wanted to marry her. It didn't mean she would screw him over, or make him sign over the family fortune, or break his heart. *This* time he knew better.

'The MCG does offer all those burly footballers to ogle,' he said.

He uncurled his legs from under his chair until he hit pay dirt. Then he slowly, deliberately slid his calf against hers. Her breath caught, but she didn't pull away. Meaning she was either strong-willed, or as into him as he was into her. Knowing his luck, she was both.

She picked up her glass of wine and took a long sip. Then said, 'Alas, that isn't enough of an inducement. We have footballers aplenty in Paris. Burly ones, even. I know several personally through the magazine.'

His calf-sliding operation hit a standstill. Personally? Of course she did. Surely in her line of work she met so many gorgeous men she didn't know what to do with them. He found himself praying ninety per cent of them were gay. Leaving her ten per cent to play with? Even that ate at him like a poison turning his blood hot.

'Fine,' he said. 'Paris has footballers aplenty. And a big tower. And more pet stores than gelatarias. But your family is here. I know mine fretted like crazy when I went overseas and that was only for my gap year.'

'I…I don't have any close family left,' she said, suddenly sliding her leg away from his and out of reach. He noticed that her wineglass shook slightly as she put it back onto the table. 'That's why I left in the first place.'

'But Barton—'

'I had never met.' She ran a hand through her hair, mussing up the waves until she looked as if she had just rolled out of bed. He shifted on his seat. And admitted that the fancy dress was nothing more than window-dressing. She was so effortlessly sexy no matter what she wore. He ached to know just how sexy she might be wearing nothing at all.

'Look, can we talk about something else?' she asked.

'Sure. No family,' he said. 'And no business. I guess all that leaves is gossip. So, tell me more about those you left pining for you in Paris.'

She shook her head, and ducked her chin, until her hair fell over her face and she was hidden behind a veil of disorderly waves. 'Nobody in Paris pines for me.

Except maybe my boss's shih-tzu. I worry she's remembered to feed the poor thing without me to remind her.'

'Now you're just trying to get me to feel all sorry for you so I'll promise not to set the Cosgroves on you again.'

Her mouth creased into a sexy half-smile. 'I'm not living in the kind of world where people pine for other people. It's the quick and the dead. The avant-garde versus last year's cast-offs. Out of sight out of mind.'

He leaned forward, resting his chin on his palm. In the muted light her hair seemed a thousand different colours. The hollows beneath her fine cheekbones were dark and, oh, so feminine. And her lips shone, covered as they were in the faintest layer of gloss, which she hadn't yet managed to bite completely away. He wondered how a woman like this could believe she could so easily slip from anyone's mind, even if she was thousands of miles away.

'Right,' he said. 'Though I was looking for something along the lines of Parisian footballers. And pining. And any combination thereof.'

'Oh.' Her green eyes flickered as she caught his meaning. Flickered and warmed. Like freshly cut emeralds. 'There's no pining on that front either, I'm sure.'

'Mmm. You know what? I wouldn't count on it. We guys can pine pretty well without letting on. We learn the healing power of pining about the same time we learn why we want to pull on girls' pigtails.'

Saxon saw his chance and took it. He reached out, wrapping a lock of her soft hair around his fingers, then tugged, before letting the waves fall through his fingers, the delicate strands tickling his knuckles with such a sweet caress he wished he hadn't been so hasty in letting go after all. He wished he had pushed his fingers deeper into her hair, along her scalp, until her waves tumbled over his wrists and her eyes fell closed from the pleasure of it.

Those same wide green eyes now bore into his. Wide, liquid, dazzling eyes. Eyes that made him want to give up steak, soufflé and Sav Blanc and just get the hell out of here with her at his side. In his arms. In his bed.

He was ready to throw it all to the wind and give into temptation, to touch her in a way so as not to arouse the suspicions of the other diners while arousing her to the point where she could no longer feel her toes; she was saved by the fact that her purse began to sing. And vibrate. And jump around the table as her mobile phone rang.

He sat back and folded his arms. His ringtone was Sinatra's 'That's Life'. Her taste seemed to run to god-awful, doof doof, deep base, dance party song. Maybe he was the one who'd just been saved.

Morgan scrambled for her purse. It was work. Or more precisely her impossible assistant, Leon. The picture staring back at her, one he had so kindly loaded into her phone and she had no idea how to remove, was of a skinny kid in Elvis Costello glasses, leather pants and a hot-pink crushed velvet shirt drinking a daiquiri. And while if she'd been anywhere else she would have thrown her phone across the room, or drowned the noise beneath her pillow, she dived for the answer button as though it were a life raft.

'Sorry,' she whispered to Saxon, 'I have to get this. I won't be long.'

She shot from her chair and made her way back

through the tables to an out-of-the-way spot near the entrance to the bar. 'Leon,' she said between clenched teeth. 'What on earth are you calling me for?'

'Morgan, sweetie, you're alive,' he said in his plummy British accent.

'Of course I'm alive, Leon. Leaving Paris doesn't mean you die.' She glanced back across the restaurant at Saxon, somewhat glad she hadn't said that in front of him. He would certainly have used it against her. As she watched Saxon checked his watch. He appeared not at all happy about the intrusion. Well, he could get in line. His unhappiness had nothing on hers.

'Tell me what's up. I'm busy. And I'm on leave.'

'Well, you haven't been answering your cell phone so I became all worried. I didn't know where you were staying so I went through your Filofax and found your mother's number and called her to see if you were there.'

Morgan felt her blood leave her face. Damn, damn, damn! Now she would have to call Pamela. And to wring Leon's skinny neck and leave him in a dark alley somewhere. She moved deeper into the alcove until she was all but sitting in a huge potted plant.

'You called my mother?' she snapped. 'Alicia knows where I'm staying. She has managed to get a good half-dozen messages to my room. You didn't think to check with her first?'

'Second. I checked with her second. And then I rang your mum to let her know where you were staying since you'd obviously forgotten.'

'Morgan?'

Morgan spun around to find Saxon behind her. So big. So tall. So much man compared with the kid with drawn-on eyebrows whom she was clinging to right now. She shrank further into the plant.

'Whoa there. Is everything okay?' Saxon asked.

She held her hand over the mouthpiece. 'Fine. It's work. I won't be long.'

He reached out and touched her arm. Her bare arm. Rays of heat spiralled outward from his touch. 'The entrées have arrived.'

'Right, okay. I'll be back in a sec.'

He smiled. Ran his hand up her arm, then brushed a lock of hair from her shoulder. She swayed towards him as he turned and walked away.

'Now is *that* the reason you had to run off in the middle of the night, leaving poor Alicia in a tizz to end all tizzes?' Leon asked.

'Sorry?' she asked, then realised her hand was still over the mouthpiece. 'What was that?'

'The man with the ocean-deep voice. And the cooling entrées.'

'Yes. I mean no. No, he's not. It's just business.'

'Please tell me you mean monkey business.'

'Leon, please tell *me* why you rang, right now, or the second I see you again I will, and I am not kidding here, I will hurt you.'

'Alicia made me.'

'She what? Why?'

'She has work she wants you to do.'

'Work. No. I can't. I've taken annual leave. That means that I am currently unavailable for work.'

'Okay, so I lied about the work.' He sighed dramatically. 'She keeps asking me when you are coming home. Put me out of my misery and give me a date.'

Home. That word was sure springing up a great deal

nowadays. Morgan ran her fingers through her hair. 'I can't do this now, Leon, okay? I have things to sort out here that require my complete concentration.'

'I don't blame you. He sounds delicious. My advice? Don't be your usual grim self. Smile more. Men like that.'

She hung up the phone with a snap.

After a couple of deep breaths, she turned to find Saxon at the other end of the restaurant, leaning back in his chair, looking smooth and cool and at ease. A waitress was pouring him another glass of wine. He said something and the waitress laughed, and tossed her hair and pulled her shoulders back. When she walked away there was a definite sway to her hips.

Morgan took a deep breath, and fixed her dress, which was suddenly feeling dishevelled. She shook out her hair, which always looked dishevelled no matter what she did, and made her way back towards the table.

When she was halfway through the room, he looked up and caught her eye. Her heart skipped a beat. He smiled and it skipped another. She reminded herself that he was *not* in fact the reason she was in town.

He *was* the reason her skin vibrated, her fingers trembled, and her breaths felt heavier with each closer step. He was the reason she was wearing a dress that practically whispered the word 'sex' every time it swished against her legs. And he was the reason she wouldn't be going back to work any earlier than the weekend.

Consequently when she reached the table she grabbed her purse and said, 'I have to go.'

'Now?' he asked, his eyes tinged with concern. 'Are you sure everything's okay?'

'Sure. Kind of. Not really. It was my assistant, Leon,

on the phone. There are problems at work. I have to go sort them out.'

'Eat first,' he said. 'Sort later.'

She glanced at the beautiful-looking entrée and her stomach threatened to grumble. But Leon's call was a sign. Her focus was split. Her career was paramount because her independence was important to her. And until her inheritance was sorted out her continued employment hung on the whim of a woman who thought hair scrunchies were retro cool. Emotional attachments to *people*, on the other hand, only got in the way. She'd learned her lesson young. *Nothing* was fair in love and war.

'I have to go now,' she said again.

Saxon threw his serviette to the table and stood, moving nearer her. Morgan pulled her chair between them. Her focus was keen enough she knew she ought to keep physical distance as well as emotional from this one particular man.

'You can't leave him to sort things out in your stead?' he asked, his voice low, intimate, suggestive.

She took another step back. 'That's right. I can't.'

'Surely he must realise that you have your hands full sorting out your grandfather's estate.' He placed his hands on the back of her chair and leaned in, surrounding her in his cinnamon aroma.

She let go of the chair and shook her head. 'He doesn't know that's why I'm here.'

His eyebrows shot skyward, his little seduction act all but forgotten. 'You didn't tell your assistant that your grandfather died?'

She shook her head.

'Why the hell not?'

It was her turn to raise her eyebrows. 'Because even if he gave a damn it's none of his business.'

'If he's a colleague of yours then surely he cares—'

'Enough,' she shot back, holding out a hand and stopping him mid-stream. She took control of her voice before adding, 'It's not... I'm not like you, okay? I don't have a hundred and one fun stories to tell about home and hearth. I consider my private life private.'

Everything suddenly felt so quiet in the cavernous room she could hear her own strenuous breaths. If he asked *why* once more she was going to simply turn and walk away.

'So what does Leon think you are doing here?'

You, she almost said. She closed her eyes for a second to compose herself. When she opened them she decided he had moved closer. She could now see flecks of decidedly warm caramel within his dark chocolate eyes. 'He thinks I'm here on holidays, I guess.'

'It hardly sounds like you work in the warmest environment.'

'The Chic offices have central heating,' she said, tilting her head. Yep, he was definitely closer. 'That's all the warmth I need.'

'Morgan, everybody needs more warmth that that.'

No, she told herself. *You don't need more warmth. You need to walk away. You need to call Leon back. Do whatever it is Alicia wants you to do. And then tomorrow you need to meet the architects and town planners and anyone else who might be able to make this all go away as soon as humanly possible.*

She reached into her purse to find enough money to cover her half of the uneaten meal. But his hand snaked between them and took her purse and her money. He refolded the colourful notes, placed them back within and shut the clasp with care and precision. 'It was my invitation, so dinner, or lack thereof, is on me.'

Free coffees, free advice, free dinner. What would he offer next to sweeten the deal? Free love?

He held out her purse and she took it, even though it meant her fingers had to slide against his. As always his touch was electric. 'Thank you,' she said, her voice annoyingly breathy.

He nodded, bowing slightly from the waist. 'You can thank me properly by agreeing to do this again.'

'Not have dinner? Any time.'

He smiled, and her stomach did a back flip.

'Let's throw caution to the wind. Next time we have dinner, how about we actually eat?'

'I…I don't think that's a good idea.'

His smile shifted and grew. Slowly, but surely, as though he knew even she didn't believe her own words. 'And why's that?'

'We are at war, remember?'

'Mmm,' he said, the sound rumbling through the floorboards, into her shoes and up her legs until it settled around her midriff. 'Even the Germans and the English took time out from World War One for armistice on Christmas Day.'

He reached out and rested a hand against her waist. The chair was no longer in between them. When she took another step back she found herself up against the cold glass window. 'Which one are you meant to be?' she asked.

'The goodie, of course,' he said. Then his other hand reached out and lay flat against the glass. She looked over his shoulder, hoping for someone to rescue her, to run in and say, 'We'll have none of that here,' but everyone, even the blondes, brunettes and the redhead had found something to occupy them in that moment.

She took in a deep breath and let it out as slowly and surreptitiously as she could. 'Doesn't that depend which side you are on? If both sides claim right is on their side, they can't both be accurate.'

'No, they can't. That's why you're the baddie.' His mouth, which was suddenly mere centimetres from hers, kicked into a smile and her knees turned to jelly.

She didn't claim to be right; all she'd ever wanted to be was all right. And if that meant raising the rent by fifty per cent or knocking the Como Avenue down, and dressing gaudy sets with fake flamingos and fake plants for Alicia, and babysitting Leon while she was meant to be on annual leave, well, that was just what she'd have to do.

Saxon's warm breath tickled at the hair trailing down her breastbone. He was kidding if he thought himself the goodie. He was just plain bad. Bad, and hazardous to her health. And if she didn't extricate herself, and soon, she was afraid he might convince her not only to see him again socially, but to see him socially for the rest of the night.

His hand slid further around her back. Her breath shot out of her in a great whoosh as he took the weight of her. And she let him. There was just something so warm, and affable, and cocky, and sure that got to her. Whether it spoke to the echo of a laid-back, easygoing, 'she'll be right' Australian within her, or simply the *woman* within her, she had no idea. All she knew was that it connected, and deep. In a cap and apron he was

sexy, but in a suit and clean-shaven he made her brain
turn to mush.

Well, she couldn't afford mushy brain. She was still
jet-lagged, she was further behind in her quest to sort
out her grandfather's building than she had been when
she'd arrived, her mother now knew she was in town,
and Leon and Alicia were falling apart.

Her eyes squeezed shut tight against the onslaught,
and suddenly she felt trapped. Uncommon emotion and
helpless inevitability swarmed down upon her. She
needed fresh air. Her bohemian blood insisted upon it.
Truth and beauty, she never lacked in her life. Freedom
was her constant struggle.

And you can't forget love, a little voice in the back
of her head whispered. *Run as far as you like, but it is
in your blood to love as strongly as your father loved.
And in your history to have it turned to garbage the
minute you turn your back.*

She grabbed a hold of the last threads of her will-
power and slipped sideways and beneath his arm.
Saxon's hand slid off her waist and she was free. She
almost whimpered with relief.

'Good night, Saxon,' she said, stepping further away
from him with every word.

He leant a hand against the back of what had been
her chair and crossed his legs at the ankle. Easy as you
please. Seemingly not even one tenth as affected as she
was. But his heavy breathing and dark hot eyes gave
him away. 'It doesn't have to be that way,' he said.

'Yes,' she said, her voice so husky she barely recognised it. 'It does.'

And though everything inside her, every lonely, shel-
tered, pressed-down place inside her that was suddenly

blooming, and reaching back to him, screamed at her to give into the look in his eyes, to whatever time, and smiles and pleasure the guy would afford her, even if it was only for a few, brief, splendiferous days, she turned and walked away.

Knowing full well that, as well as a large bed far too big for one small person, there would be a message from her mother waiting for her in her room.

CHAPTER FOUR

LATE the next morning the bell over the front door of Bacio Bacio tinkled. The party noise inside the gelataria didn't abate in the slightest. Uncle Georgio continued his rant about Berlusconi, and the Felangi twin toddlers ran into one another head first and were screaming up a storm.

Someone must have forgotten to lock the front door again, the 'Private Function' sign would never be enough to turn away regular customers and family always used the back door. Saxon's gaze flickered over the crowd of heads until he found the first unfamiliar one.

His mouth kicked into a grin when he realised it wasn't nearly as unfamiliar as he'd first thought. Wearing a beige newsboy cap, her long hair again hanging in wilting waves over her shoulders, a short navy pea coat, and skinny jeans tucked into knee-high red boots, Morgan Kipling-Rossetti made him feel as ravenous as he had the night before, and not for food.

Cousin Angelo spotted her a good three seconds later. *'Ciao, bella!'* he cried out, approaching her with arms open wide, earning him a few dirty glances from the younger cousins who had to duck out of the way.

Morgan's down-turned mouth set into a deeper

frown as she took on a kind of Lara Croft action: feet shoulder-width apart, slow-turning body, eyes taking in every possible escape route. Angelo did the smart thing and stopped in his tracks.

'Is Saxon here?' he heard her ask over the noise of fifty-odd Ciantars mid-party.

'Of course she wants Saxon,' Angelo said on a sigh. 'You know, there was a time when Angelo was king. Now the young prince has come into his own.'

Angelo turned and disappeared into the crowd. Morgan watched him for a few bemused moments before taking a deep breath and edging her way through his boisterous family.

Saxon stepped out in front of her. 'Fancy seeing you here.'

'Saxon,' she said on a soft release of breath. The pleasure behind her sigh did crazy things to his insides. But her recent Lara Croft impersonation was fresh in his mind so he did the smart thing and put his hands into his pockets instead of anywhere near her.

She put a finger in her right ear and squinted. 'What's going on here?'

'Aunt Tina's birthday party. We're actually closed.'

'I saw the sign.' She motioned towards the front door with a hand that held a cup of coffee from a nearby competitor. Cheeky little so-and-so.

He ignored it for the moment and leant against the wall. 'But still you just had to have a shot of lime gelato. I get that. When the craving takes you…'

Her eyes flickered to glimpses of shiny glass at the far end of the room as though she had forgotten they were even there. 'Ah, no. I came to see you.'

'Well, that's flattering, to be sure, especially when

compared with the standard of my gelato. Maybe you should try some. Make the comparison honest. That way I can be sure you're really into me for me.'

'I'm not *into you*, Saxon,' she said, though her eyes shifted away from his right at the last moment. 'I just need to talk.'

'We'll see.' He took her by the hand, tucking it beneath his arm as he shepherded her through the crowd to the counter where Trisha was manning the scoop, handing out mounds of chilled heaven to the kids.

He snagged the coffee cup from Morgan's hand and threw it into a bin behind the counter.

'Hey. I wasn't done with that,' she said, bending over the counter so far he thought she might follow it in. He grabbed her around the waist and pulled her to safety, which happened to bring her flush against him, her hands flat against his chest.

She blinked up at him, and he stared down at her.

'Oh, yeah, you were,' he said.

Again she smelt of black cherries: tart and sweet all at once. And again, just like that, he was spellbound. It seemed eating dinner alone, followed by a cold shower and a lonely night in his big bed, hadn't cooled his attraction to the woman one bit.

When she began to unconsciously melt against him he felt things stirring down below that he didn't think entirely appropriate for the venue. He gently set her aside and spun her to face the gelato, but he kept his hand resting lightly against her back, marking his place.

'Now which one takes your fancy?' he asked. 'Chocolate? No, that's far too common. Strawberry? Nah, too sweet for the kind of person who purposely brings another man's coffee. Hazelnut?'

She screwed up her nose.

'No? A woman who doesn't like hazelnut. Aren't you just one in a million?'

'Aren't I just. Now, Saxon, can we please just—?'

'No. Choose. Taste. Then we talk.'

'Fine! If that's what it will take.' She turned back to peruse the colourful array without any discernible interest. It really was the dandiest thing. He supplied something women the world over would kill to get their hands on, but this woman didn't give a hoot. Conversely it only made him want her more.

She opened her mouth to say something, but he pressed a finger against her lips. Her eyes grew wide, creating a strange kind of thump behind his ribs. But it was her mouth that quickly had him enthralled. Her lips lay soft and warm beneath his finger, the crush of teeth behind them creating all sorts of visions of exactly how that mouth would feel beneath his own.

He pulled his finger away, and pressed it up against his mouth just long enough to say, 'Shh.' And just long enough to taste the remaining warmth planted there from her lips. 'Trisha,' he said, *'mi ottiene una paletta del gelato del caffè.'*

Trisha proceeded to gather a good-sized dollop of the flavour Saxon had suggested before smearing it into a small red tub. Once in hand, he took a small, flat-ended, plastic spoon from the receptacle, scooped up a bite-sized mound, and held it out to Morgan. 'Did you know gelato was created in fifteen sixty-five at the court of Medici by a Florentine gourmet called Bernado Buontalenti? He figured out how to freeze churned sweetened milk and egg yolks.'

'Egg yolks?' She stared at the spoon. 'You're kidding me, right?'

'I promise,' he said, 'you've never had better.'

She blinked up at him, and blushed, taking his words the wrong way. Or the right way. Depending how one chose to look at it. Saxon chose to breathe deeper to fill his suddenly empty lungs.

Finally, with a resigned breath she opened her mouth. Saxon slid the spoon inside. Neat white teeth and soft pink lips scraped over the spoon and never in his whole life had he been as jealous of an inanimate object. He watched in enraptured silence as she let the gelato melt and sink into the crevices of her mouth, breathing through her nose as the flavours slithered over her taste buds.

'So what do you think?' he asked.

'It was coffee-flavoured, right?' she asked, her cheek lifting into a half-smile.

He nodded.

'You're right,' she said. 'I've never had better.'

'Not as effusive an admission as I'm used to.'

She gave a small shrug. 'It was nice. But I'd prefer the real thing any day. Sorry.'

The truth of that statement hit him like an arrow through the chest. For what it meant was she really was into him purely for him. Dammit. He never should have let her leave the night before.

She waved a hand in front of him, her brow furrowing. 'Now can we go somewhere else to talk?'

'What's wrong with here?' Saxon said, knowingly licking the last remnants of coffee gelato off her spoon.

She glanced about the room, and only then did he notice mild panic skipping across the jade-green depths of her eyes. She was afraid of being lynched.

'Relax,' he said. 'Nobody else here knows about you. *Yet.*'

She swallowed, the muscles in her fine neck working overtime. 'Thank you. I appreciate it.'

Her words were sweet, soft and true. Enough that the arrow in his chest dissolved and floated away, leaving his heart open to her. He had no intention of becoming exposed like this. Attracted, fine. Desperate with desire, great! But vulnerable to the shift and fall of a woman's pretty throat, that was bad, *bad* news.

'Don't think I'm protecting *you*, honey,' he said, serious for the first time since she'd walked through his door. 'If they knew who you were and why you were here it would just kill them.'

Her eyes narrowed, all evidence of sweetness vaporised. *Much better.* 'Then it would seem best for both of us if we went somewhere a little more private.'

Now private sounded good. Unfortunately private in this place meant a two-by-two-metre office so filled with boxes only one person could sit down at a time. He'd love to build a bigger office on site one day if only Barton... No. This slip of a woman had the power now. She had the power to let him build into the car park, and she had the power to take his car park away. It was time to hear what she had to say.

He lifted a portion of the counter and waved her through. She slid past, bathing him in her cherry scent. He barely held back his groan. If she was carrying whipped cream and icing sugar on her person she might just be his perfect woman.

'Through the brown door,' he said, his voice gruff.

He followed close behind and closed the office door behind him, muffling the sounds of the party. He stepped over boxes of serviettes and logo-imprinted paper cups until he found a patch of clear floor. Which happened to be right beside the same patch of floor Morgan was on. She spun in the small space, but there was nowhere else to go. One more step forward, by either of them, and they would be in one another's arms.

Nervous eyes darted up to meet his and the small room suddenly seemed airless. And he wasn't the only one who felt it. Her chest rose and fell as though she'd run a mile. Her pupils grew darker and bigger by the second. Oh, yeah, she was into him, no matter how hard she protested. And he was definitely into her.

Only one thing he knew to do about that… He leant in, her delicious scent wrapping itself around him. Up close he noticed that her right eyebrow was slightly askew, and several pale freckles dusted her dainty nose. For some reason those small imperfections made his heart race all the faster.

Then as his lips opened, ready to press against hers, she shook her head. Just once. But it was enough to slam him to a full stop.

His hesitation was all she needed. In one blink of those luscious eyes, all evidence of the soft, sweet, luscious, kissable woman was gone and in her place was a whirlwind of potential energy that sent him rocking back onto his heels.

'Saxon,' she said, her voice overly loud. 'I'm here because this letter was pushed under my hotel-room door when I got back from my appointment with my ar-chitect this morning.'

She waved a flat piece of paper between them so fast he couldn't catch a word of it. But he knew what it was. He leant back, sat on the edge of the small desk, and crossed his arms. 'I thought it only fair to let you know we have applied for heritage listing of the building.'

She threw her arms in the air now that she had the space to do so. 'How? This place is a dump. I mean, look at this room. There's rot in the ceiling, the floor tiles are broken. And this is the best of the lot. This is nothing more than a blatant attempt to stall time.'

'So say you,' Saxon said.

'So would say any sane person. And while we're on the subject, a sane person would realise that this place is mine and I can do with it as I please. A sane person wouldn't go to the depths of trotting out tearful people of retirement age to try to tug on my heartstrings. I may not be from around here any more, I may not know the secret passwords to get things done in this city, but one thing I do know is that I don't like surprises. The more you push me, Saxon, the harder I will push back.'

Her eyes blazed, her cheeks grew pink, and a vein in her forehead began to pulse. She was so fired up it was actually kind of daunting. And Saxon had never been more turned on in his whole life.

If it weren't for the very real threat of sustaining multiple paper cuts, he would have taken that opportunity to let her know just how far he was willing to push her to get what he wanted. The problem was, the precise details of what he wanted were starting to get a little fuzzy.

He wanted Bacio Bacio untouched. He wanted his friends, they who had sent as much business his way as they could during the lean times after his divorce, looked after. But more and more he also wanted Morgan Kipling-Rossetti. A woman with far too many surnames, far too many fancy clothes, and far too many miles between his home and hers for any kind of relationship to come of it...

Saxon pulled on his mental breaks. The *last* thing he wanted was a *relationship*. He'd tried that before and failed spectacularly. And he was a guy who didn't take failure well, as evidenced by the fact that when he'd hung onto his disastrous marriage as long as he had in order to avoid failure at all costs it had almost cost him everything else.

One thing he'd learnt was that sometimes giving up was the right thing to do. The trick, the skill, the *talent* was weeding out what one truly wanted most and giving up the rest without regret.

'So that's it,' he said. 'That's all you came here to tell me.'

'Well, yes. Pretty much.' Her bravado faltered.

'And you couldn't have done it over the phone?'

She blinked, ten to the dozen. 'I...I was infuriated—still am, in fact. I came here to ask you to stop playing games, and to suggest we sort this thing out like adults.'

Saxon stuck out his bottom lip and nodded. 'You caught a cab?'

Her eyes flickered in confusion. 'Well, yes.'

'And you let the cabbie go.'

'Of course I did.'

'So you'll need a lift home now that you're done here.'

She shook her head. 'What I need is a phone. To call another cab. So if you don't mind...' She reached for the phone on Darius's desk.

But Saxon got there first. When her hand landed upon his it leapt away as though burnt. She quickly tucked it and the letter into the deep pocket of her navy coat.

'Let me take you back to your hotel,' he said. 'We can talk on the way. Like adults.'

She opened her mouth to protest. But he saw the moment she realised he had trapped her in her own rhetoric. Her brow furrowed and pretty mouth turned down at the corners as he was fast learning it was wont to do. 'But don't you have to stay for the rest of the party?'

'They won't miss me. Besides, soon there will be singing. And Lambrusco. And if I don't get out of here now I never will.'

She glanced past him, to the sounds of laughter and merriment. When she looked back at him her eyes were still bright from the battle, but she no longer looked as though she wanted to hit him over the head with Darius's stapler.

'If you give me a lift, I will be releasing you from Lambrusco and singing,' she said.

He nodded. 'Spot on.'

'So I'd be doing you a favour,' she said.

He nodded again, this time more slowly.

'And then you'll owe me,' she said.

His head stopped mid-nod as his trap turned to spring back on him. He made to protest, then stopped himself. Another thing his divorce had taught him was that if he had to lose a battle or two to win the war, then so be it. He'd done what he had to do to keep Bacio Bacio intact at that time, and he would do the same now. 'I will owe you,' he agreed.

'I will make you pay up,' she said, poking him in the chest.

'I look forward to it.' He lifted himself away from the desk and moved around the boxes to open the door.

The raucous noise from the party reverberated in the small room, and the last remaining threads of intimacy slipped away. He held out a hand so that she had no choice but to slide past him. Her soft curves bumped against him, lighting several spot fires within.

At some stage the party had grown, so much so that half the crowd were now in the kitchen. Ciantars were everywhere. Morgan turned right, when he needed her to turn left, so he reached out and slid his arm around her waist and led her where he needed her to go.

Family members kissed cheeks and called out loud goodbyes. Her hand locked his against her waist, as though if he let her go she would drown in the sea of people.

'Hang on,' he whispered against her hair, then he shifted places, and pulled her around until her back was flush against his front, and tucked his pointer fingers over hers to let her know he would not let her go.

They made their way towards the back door thus. When his right leg moved forward so did hers. The rise and fall of her buttocks against the front of his jeans was almost more than he could bear.

By the time they made it outside, he was so turned on she had to have known it. She pulled away from him. He glanced at her as he passed. Her eyes skittered to his, caught and held. 'Are we even yet?' he asked, his voice husky, his breath white on the cold winter air.

She laughed, not even beginning to pretend she hadn't noticed how erotic their walk together had been. 'Not even close.'

He took her hand, and she let him. Together they skirted the twenty-odd cars jammed together atop the cracked pavement out the back of the shops. Saxon had

been one of the last to arrive, so his car had a clear run
down the driveway. He pulled his keys from his back
pocket and opened the passenger side door.

'This is yours?' she asked, leaning over to peer
into Bessie's window at real leather seats and a wood-
grain dashboard.

Saxon's eyes roved over the gentle dark blue curves
of his favourite lady friend. Though when they met the
dark blue curves of Morgan's tilted backside they didn't
move an inch further. 'Morgan, meet Bessie. Bessie,
this is Morgan. Isn't she a beauty?'

'That she is,' Morgan said on a sigh.

When she stood up and looked his way, he was still
watching her. And he hadn't been kidding. She was
beautiful. Her hair had been slightly mussed by the
gentle winter breeze, leaving waves of delicate dark
blonde hair flicked across her chest and over her shoulders like some kind of mermaid. The newsboy cap
shaded her eyes from the weak winter sun, creating
shadows and hollows around her beautiful eyes. Her
skin had turned pale and her lips dark pink in the cold
air.

She didn't seem all that toxic in that moment. She
simply seemed lovely. Fragile perhaps, even a little
insecure, and on the other side of the looking glass from
him in so many ways. But lovely.

He had to kiss her. Just once. To taste the promise
he'd held on the tip of his finger. He wanted to savour
her lips with the scent of black cherry in his nose, the
flavour of caffè gelato on her tongue, and use her
warmth to stave off the winter chill rocketing through
his indoor clothes.

He stepped towards her. She backed up against his

car, arching back over Bessie's gentle curves. He reached out to her and this time she didn't flinch. She let him run a hand over her hair. It was so soft, trailing over his fingers, fine as silk. If he didn't know better, if he hadn't witnessed that quick temper of hers, he would have thought her the most delicate woman he'd ever met. Fine-boned, translucent skin, and those big glossy eyes, framed by whisper-thin lashes. *Exquisite.*

'Morgan,' he said, letting her name roll across his tongue.

'Yes, Saxon.' She tilted her chin as if to say she was ready, as though nothing he did could ever truly get to her. But when her hand fluttered to rest against his chest he could feel her trembling.

He brought his hands to either side of her face. His wrists almost touched at the end of her dainty chin. Then finally, finally, finally he leaned down and, with a sigh as soft as a guy his size could manage, he kissed her.

And this time Morgan didn't do a thing to stop him.

She'd tried, any number of times since she'd first laid eyes on him. To cork these unwelcome feelings. To ignore this intoxicating need. There were a million different reasons why she still should. But now, as Saxon's mouth touched hers, hot and supple and masterful, she couldn't remember one of them.

She let her eyes drift closed as his lips moved relentlessly over her own. As his thumbs stroked softly against her cheek, down her neck, into the sensitive hollow of her *décolletage.*

Desire washed over her. She wasn't sure if it was hers, his or a heady, hazy mixture of both. Either way her hand clenched a hold of his sweater. Tight. Her fingers fisting around a mound of dark, soft wool. To keep him close and to keep the slightest gap between them. Her stomach clenched so as not to give in completely and simply melt against the wall of warm muscle.

His hands stole around the back of her head, tucking deep within her hair, tugging, massaging her scalp. Bliss. And as every numb place inside her began to thaw she gave in and slid her arms over his broad shoulders and around his neck, diving into the hair at the base of his neck.

He was so big. So broad. She stood as high on her tiptoes as she could manage to get closer. Deeper. Picking up on her desperation, he tilted just enough for his kisses to become more insistent. His tongue slid into her mouth, toying with hers. He wrapped his arms about her and held her tight. So tight she could barely breathe. And the more he gave her, the more she wanted.

The cold metal of the car threatened to seep through her denim. She waited for it to burn, but it merely melted away before it hit skin. For her skin was out of her control. Warmed as it was from the hot, thudding pulse of her blood coursing too fast through her veins. She could no longer feel anything bar every millimetre of her that connected with him. The soft fabric of his sweater beneath her palm. His massaging fingers digging into her waist. The sexy rasp of his stubble against her chin. And his, oh, so talented mouth. She clung to it as if it were everything to her, air and energy and sustenance all.

Eons later Saxon slowed, his lips teasing hers as his kisses became softer, gentler, fewer, and further between. Until finally they stopped. He leaned his forehead against hers. And the sound of their laboured breaths echoed within the cocooned space between them.

'Your heart's beating so fast,' she said.

'Your fault entirely,' he said, his sexy deep voice rumbling through her.

He lifted his head, shook his hair off his face and looked down at her. His eyes were murky and filled with ruffled emotions. With surprise. And with dark depths of unquenched desire as he drank her in. She wondered if he saw the same feelings in her.

She swallowed down the lump of desire clogging her throat. It wasn't at all like her to be this way. She was careful not to make an impact, and people didn't make an impact on her. For it simply hurt her too much when such people left. She still had a soul-deep hole inside herself from when the father she had adored had died. A hole that nine years in Paris, his home town, hadn't yet managed to fill.

But somehow she had let down her defences just long enough to let this man make an impact. In less than twenty-four hours a body-length imprint of him lingered on her senses. And it terrified her. 'We shouldn't have let that happen,' she said.

'Who says?'

'I say. Common sense says. It complicates things. And things are already far too complicated for my comfort.'

'Comfort schomfort.' Saxon lifted his hand, trailing his fingers along her cheek before gently pushing a swathe of hair away from her neck. 'I'd give up comfort for the chance to do this to you any day.'

Her eyes grew heavy. Her limbs lax. 'And what

happens when your family does find out who I am? Do you think they'll be so understanding?'

'Believe me, Morgan, this has nothing to do with that. This has everything to do with the fact that your skin is just so damn soft. And smooth. And as it turns out I have far less will-power than I thought I had.'

He leant in, slowly, giving her the chance to pull away. To stop him. To say no for real. But when she didn't move, when she stood-stock still, her breaths gaining momentum, he smiled.

But his cruel mouth left her lips alone as he followed the trail his fingers had burned into her skin, pressing against the delicate point where her neck met her shoulder. Then just below her ear. Then the edge of her cheek.

He pulled away. An inch. Until his mouth was so close to hers she could taste him. His hot breath whispering against her lips. She could feel them swell and throb, the agony of waiting for him to touch her there again burned. She'd never experienced anything like it.

But he didn't move. Not back or forward. All the while she so ached to kiss him. Ached until she couldn't stand it any longer. As it turned out his will-power was far stronger than hers. She tilted her chin, lifted back onto her toes, and their lips met.

The gently insistent kiss of earlier was a thing of the past. This time, the moment their lips met, a kaleidoscope of colour and light burst behind her eyes. Fireworks went off in her stomach. Her toes lost all feeling as her blood rushed north.

Saxon's strong hands took her around the waist, hauling her away from the car to mesh against his length. His knee sliding between her thighs, opening her to him. She clamped her legs around his with every last vestige of power her slack limbs could summon.

She wrapped her arms around his broad back, sliding along the beltline of his jeans, untucking his T-shirt in three desperate yanks, until her cold fingertips were scraping delectably against hot skin.

The muscles of his back clenched at the sudden touch, the sudden chill. The feel of the wholly masculine warmth and shifting musculature beneath her hands made her groan.

He took advantage of her open mouth and plundered it with his tongue. Wrapping hers in delicious knots, teaching her ways and means and pleasures she hadn't even imagined existed within the confines of a first— or was this already their second—kiss.

And she was lost. Completely and utterly lost. To sensation, and desire and romantic, starry-eyed, idealistic rapture. The kind she'd kept at arm's length all her life, for fear it never really existed and she would only be disappointed all over again.

A horn beeped. Faraway. Or maybe it was right next to her. She was so far gone into a world of pure, unadulterated pleasure she had no idea.

But it was enough to drag her kicking and screaming into the present. She tore her hands from beneath Saxon's sweater, disentangled herself from his kiss, from his thigh, from his rapturous embrace.

She opened her eyes, and squinted against the bright white winter sunlight to find they were still somehow magically alone in the car park.

'And why are we stopping?' Saxon asked, pulling back enough to look down into her eyes, but his hands remained very much attached to her hips, his thumbs slowly sliding beneath her jacket and caressing her stomach with each word.

She bit her lip to stop from grinning like an idiot. But that was all she felt like doing. Glowing, and smiling, and lying down and sleeping for days. Taking advantage of the fact that her whole body felt as if it had had a three-hour massage.

'I told you we should never have started,' she said.

'Rubbish,' Saxon said. 'Why are we really stopping?'

'Because we are in a public car park. Because we barely know one another. Because we are at war. Because I'm not entirely sure that I even like you all that much.'

Saxon laughed. Deep, easy, relaxed, confident laughter. It was just such a sexy sound Morgan bit her lip to stop herself groaning again. 'You like me plenty,' he said. Then used the leverage of his wide hands on her hips to pull her back to him. 'And I think it's fair to say I like you too.'

Morgan's eyes fluttered so that she could concentrate on the utterly indulgent sensation of knowing without a doubt that such a gorgeous man was so attracted to her. 'I feel like I'm in a Bond movie,' she thought, then blushed when she realised she'd said it out loud.

'Why is that?' he asked before bending down to run a trail of hot, sweet kisses along her neck.

The obvious fact that he still hadn't had his fill of her gave her a huge rush of power. She tipped her head sideways to give him better access. 'Because I'm certain you are seducing me for your own ends, as part of your five-day plan to present your case.'

She felt him smile against her skin before his hot breath slid against her ear. 'Is it working?'

A voluptuous shiver rocked her body. 'Not in the least.' With a groan she rolled away from him, pulled herself back together, and took two steps away from the car. When she turned back, Saxon's hair had deep grooves from where her fingers had run through it. His mouth was moist. His T-shirt was untucked and hanging crushed beneath his sweater. Had she really done all that?

After one long moment in which he was obviously considering whether their session was really and truly over with, he ran one hand over his hair, used the other to tuck himself back in, and blew hot air over his lips to dry them. And just like that, in three quick moves he was back to normal. As though nothing had happened.

Whereas she felt branded, as though anyone would see in her eyes what she had been through. She had the horrible feeling a shower, a facial scrub and a long sleep wouldn't do a thing to erase the effects of that kiss.

She shook her hair off her shoulders, and put her hands in the tight front pockets of her jeans. 'So are you still taking me home, or was this all some elaborate ruse to get me out here to your lair?'

Saxon glanced over her shoulder at the cold, unattractive surrounds, then back to her, his mouth sliding into a debilitating half-smile. 'If this place worked that well for us, I can only imagine what we could achieve with four walls and some real privacy.'

'Let's not think past a fifteen-minute car ride.'

Saxon's eyes darkened, and his smile kicked wider.

'To my hotel. Where I will go up to my room alone. And where I will be putting in a phone call to the heritage-listing place to tell them what a shyster you in fact are.'

His smile eased, only a shadow remaining. But even that shadow, that hint, was enough to keep her heart rate from returning to a normal pace.

What was she still doing here? Trading shots? She *should* get back to her hotel. Back to her pile of papers. To more messages from Alicia. And Leon. And perhaps even from her mother, considering she hadn't yet answered the one Pamela had left the night before. The one she'd listened to a dozen times over, trying to decide if it was apologetic, reproachful, or passive-aggressive. Or if 'we would love to see you after all this time Morgan' really meant just that.

Maybe *that* was why she'd kissed the guy, in an effort to put off all the things she didn't want to face back home. There. That was a much better reason than the thought that she was so into him it made her chest hurt.

'Shall we?' she said.

Saxon reached out and pulled open the heavy car door. 'Your chariot awaits, my lady.'

She slid past him and into the bulky but comfortable seat of the classic car, and did up her old-fashioned seat belt.

He leaned in. 'Just so you know, the offer for pizza on my lounge-room floor stands.'

'I don't like pizza any more than I like ice cream,' she lied. Pizza sounded divine. As did the sound of his lounge-room floor. Which was why she wasn't having a bar of it.

'Fine,' he said, though his voice sounded suddenly strained, as though pizza was some kind of secret password and she'd failed. She glanced up at him then and he wasn't smiling any more. His eyes were intense.

'If you don't want pizza, I can do fine dining and candlelight. I can do dinner suits and lobster. A helicopter ride to a private winery. Tickets to the opera. In Sydney. You say the word and we're there.'

'I've already made arrangements for this evening,' she said, crossing her arms to fend off the chill in his voice.

His eyebrow rose. 'Arrangements?'

'You know those promises you make to people and keep.' Her only arrangements had been a loosely thought-out plan to take a nostalgic walk through the city, but still…

His eyes narrowed, their clever focus flickering over her face—over her clenched jaw, the rise and fall of her throat, her fast-blinking eyes. The intensity in his eyes faded when he laughed, though the sound was kind of sad. As if it was missing its usual undercurrent of easygoing joy.

'To tell you the truth,' he said, 'I do believe you've just let me off the hook in a big way. For the sorry truth is I'll always be happier with pizza.'

Saxon shut her door, then with a spring in his step and a whistle on his lips jogged around the front of the car. Morgan watched him feeling as though that whole conversation had gone straight over her head.

Well, the one thing they could agree on was that dinner together was best avoided. No dinner, and no more kissing, she promised herself as he hopped in the car and started the engine with a key and a button. Just business. All business. And nothing but business.

Before he turned out of the driveway and onto Como Avenue he shot her one last hot glance that she felt all the way to her toes. He shook his head and let out his next breath in a long, low whistle, then pulled out onto the empty street.

And she wondered how on earth she hoped to get through this whole damn thing unscathed.

CHAPTER FIVE

MORGAN slid the key card into her hotel room door and dragged her tired feet inside to find the hotel phone ringing.

She took off her hat and threw it on the bedside table, then shook out her hair, running frantic fingernails along her scalp. And stared at the phone. It could be any number of people, most of whom she didn't want to talk to. Or it could be the Heritage Council calling with an appointment time.

She took a deep breath and answered it.

'Morgan, sweetie!' her assistant's voice cried out.

'Leon.' She glanced at her watch. 'It's got to be midnight over there.'

'Therefore my day is just beginning.'

'True.' She kicked off her boots, then padded barefoot into the large white marble *en suite*. 'What do you want?'

'Oooee,' Leon said. 'We are in a mood. Did your boyfriend just now dump you?'

'He's not my boyfriend.'

'He, being that dashing fellow with the voice and the entrées from last night?' Leon asked.

Morgan bit her lip, realising too late she had been trapped into admitting where she was and who she was with. She tucked the phone beneath her chin, then washed her hands and ran some cold water over her face, and didn't deign to answer.

When she stood, she caught her face in the mirror. Her eyes looked huge. Her lips pink and swollen. Her cheeks were blotchy from heat flush. Twenty-odd minutes had passed, but she still looked ravaged. It was such a new look for her she couldn't help but stare.

'Leon, spit it out,' she said, placing the cold backs of her hands against her cheeks to take away the telling colour. 'Or I'll show Alicia the website résumé you've been working on. She'll have you out on your ear before you can fill your briefcase with free stuff.'

'All right already! Don't be snippy. Do you really think I want to be on the phone to you right now? When elsewhere in the city there are gorgeous men dancing without me? Alicia won't let up. She wants me to find out if you're in Melbourne on a job-hunt mission yourself.'

Morgan was so surprised she dropped the phone. It clattered into the sink. Swearing under her breath, she wiped off the worst of the water drops with a hand towel before pressing it back to her ear. 'She thinks I've come here…to stay?'

'The tug of home, my friend. It calls to all of us eventually.'

'But Paris is my home,' she said, heading back out into the bedroom. It had far better pacing shape. 'Just because I haven't completely lost my Australian accent, or bought property there, or shacked up with some French guy, well, so what? Whatever happened to *liberty* being a French value?'

'Of course it is,' Leon said, and she wondered if he was even listening any more. 'So are you coming or staying? I won't tell Alicia if you don't want me to.'

Yeah, right.

Morgan took a deep breath, and let it out slowly through her teeth. This was what she was fighting so hard to return to quickly? A boss who didn't trust her. An assistant who was as helpful as a limpet. And don't forget the family of rats visiting her Montmartre apartment had likely moved in now that she wasn't there to bang on the wall.

When that morning she'd unexpectedly fallen head over heels for the possible plans for a new Como Avenue her grandfather's architects had created. They envisaged archways throughout, French doors leading from a newly cobbled footpath into every shopfront, wall-to-wall glass inside, domed skylights on the top floor and chandeliers everywhere else. It was exactly the kind of place she herself could have dreamed up.

She stopped pacing and sat on the edge of the bed, recalling in vivid detail how she had finished off her Melbourne morning. Wrapped in a pair of warm, strong, muscular arms as a gorgeous guy kissed her senseless.

Was she really so desperate to return because Paris had stolen her heart? Or because being home brought back far too many difficult memories she'd gone to Paris to get away from in the first place? *Home.* Melbourne. The one place in the world where she still couldn't help but wear her heart on her sleeve. A place it could so easily get knocked, or bruised, or broken for good.

'Tell Alicia I'll be back in Paris within the week.'

'That's it?' Leon said.

'That's all you're getting. Perhaps I am on the lookout for a new job. Perhaps I am here to party. Or perhaps there are personal issues at stake that I don't necessarily wish to share with either of you. Leave it be, Leon, before Alicia checks your cell-phone bills and wonders why we've been chatting so long. What if she thinks I'm trying to head-hunt you too?'

'I'll see you in a week,' he said. And with that the phone line went dead.

Morgan collapsed on her back on her king-sized bed and decided she was never answering the phone ever again.

She closed her eyes and breathed through her nose. And smelled cinnamon. It lingered on her jacket. In her hair. All over her skin.

She wondered where Saxon was now. Back at the party? Heading out for lunch somewhere fabulous, or back to his home, wherever that might be, for his beloved pizza? Wherever he was, she wondered if he was thinking of her at all.

Or if her Bond-movie analogy had resonance. Could someone kiss like that, wrap someone else so tight in their embrace, without really meaning it? She knew she couldn't. She didn't have it in her to fake it. What would be the point? But Saxon? How could she possibly know?

Leon had known her for five years. And he didn't really know her at all if he had to ask if she was coming back. How could she expect to know a guy like Saxon in the space of a day? Or a week? For that was all she could give if she was going to let anything more come of this. And it was all she would get.

She let her head roll back to face the ceiling, and

something crackled under her pillow. She reached under to find a note printed on the hotel stationery.

A note saying that her mother had called twice while she was out. A note with her mother's phone number and a request to please call her back at her earliest convenience. A dull, ancient pain spread through Morgan's midriff.

She looked at the note: she looked at the phone within reach. But *that* wasn't why she was here. She could have told Leon that much at least. She crumpled the piece of paper, and threw it blindly across the room.

After dropping Morgan at her hotel, Saxon and Bessie returned to the scene of the crime. He waited for the three-year-old engine inside the forty-year-old car to purr to a halt. And sat for a moment.

His extremities still weren't even nearly back to normal. The tips of his fingers felt numb. His legs felt as though he'd run a marathon in bare feet. And the protrusion in the front of his pants hadn't a hope of settling down while he could still smell her perfume all around him. The air from the car heater seemed to bring the scent to some kind of boiling point.

He ran a hand over the stubble on his chin and tried to think of other things. Of post footy game ice baths and midwinter snow drifts and other women. Of the fact that Morgan Kipling-Rossetti was an unknown entity, a dangerous entity, an entity who lived twenty-four hours away by plane.

But none of it helped. He was enamoured. Bewitched. Her spell had woven itself around him like strands of silk: slippery, and soft. But worth the cost?

A knock came at his window. He rolled it down, and Morgan's scent slowly disappeared with the breeze.

His silver-haired father smiled down at him. The guy looked so healthy—all olive skin and bright brown eyes. Looking at him you wouldn't be able to tell he'd had a heart attack less than five years earlier.

'Hey, Sax. You coming in or going home?'

Feeling more like himself all of a sudden, Saxon got out, and gave his dad a hug. 'Who's still here?'

'Most of the young ones. Darius and your other cousins have started on the *vino*. And Dean Martin is blaring from the speakers loud enough it set off Aunt Tina's tinnitus. Your mother had to take her home. Maybe for the sake of everyone else in the neighbourhood you could ask them to turn it down.'

Saxon could. And he would. And after some good-natured ribbing they would do as he asked. He had long since proven himself the fulcrum that kept this huge family of his balanced and safe and prosperous. 'I'll stay a bit longer, then. Make sure to confiscate the keys of any who tipple too far.'

'Nowhere else you'd rather be?' his father asked.

'Are you kidding?' But as he said the words Saxon was sure he felt his nose grow. Just a little.

Vincent grinned and swung an arm around his son's neck. 'Now who was your young friend from earlier? Have we met her before?'

He shook his head.

'Pretty, I thought. Angelo certainly was very taken with her. I'd watch him if I was you.'

'No need,' Saxon said with a grin he knew looked very much like his dad's. 'I have the feeling Morgan can take care of herself on that score.'

'Right. Your mother thought she could do with some feeding, though. Girls these days. All far too skinny. Why don't you invite her over for Sunday dinner?'

'I'll think about it.' The fact that she might in fact no longer even be in the country by then niggled at the back of his mind. Niggled, and gnawed until his head hurt.

'Don't think too hard. Too much thinking leads to too much worrying about your mother and me. Worry more about your girl and her need for some pasta, okay?'

Saxon reached around and hugged his dad again before leaving him with a kiss on the cheek. '*Ciao*, Dad.'

Vincent tucked a hand behind his head and gave it a light squeeze before walking to his own car, a newer, flashier version of Saxon's, which he had bought for his dad when the business had posted its first million-dollar profit.

As his dad walked away, strong, upright, and better looking with every year that passed, he thought about telling him who Morgan really was. And asking his advice. He had run the business before Saxon had got married. Saxon could ask if he saw any way for a compromise that would give Morgan and he both what they wanted, while leaving the option of turning this thing between them into something more.

But then he remembered his dad in the hospital, the big bull of a man so frail and grey and weak and stuffed with tubes. Better to leave him in the dark. His own shoulders were broad enough to take it all. Even if it meant being busier than a bee in summer, having his head so full of figures and plans there was little room for anything else, and possibly, even likely, doing whatever it might to keep Morgan Kipling-Rossetti on the other side of the ocean.

One perverse thought clung on tight as he headed

back into the party. He'd given up everything for the business over the past few years. To make up for what he'd almost lost in the divorce. But now that everything was swinging along beautifully, how much more could be expected of him? When would enough be enough?

The next morning Morgan picked up the neat little runabout rental car she had hired for the next week— she did not want to be caught out needing a ride from Saxon again; it came with far too many strings—stuck her cooling take-away latte in the requested cup holder, and pulled out into the light morning traffic.

She'd driven on the left-hand side of the road once or twice for Alicia in London before, but this was different. This was along city streets her architect father had taken her through a thousand times pointing out his favourite architecture, places he'd designed or places he'd simply loved. Alleyways filled with avant-garde boutiques with original ceiling mouldings and charming cafés with antique tiled floors. Wrought iron balustrades, grey gothic spires, and spindly oak trees added detail to every street.

This city wasn't all bad. *It* couldn't be blamed for anything that had gone awry in her life. Melbourne had given her her first kiss, her first school art prize, her first afternoon job at a local art gallery. It had also given her the formative love of design, and colour, and elegance, and beaux arts and culture that now dominated her life. The city itself was really very lovely.

She turned up Lygon Street, passing façade upon façade of restaurants, Italian as far as the eye could see.

Morgan turned left into Como Avenue but only got about twenty feet before she had to slam her foot on the brake. There were so many patrons they had spilled out onto the street. Signs reading 'Save Our Stores' blocked off the usually dreary windows. Trestle-tables and barbecues lined the footpath hosting a sausage sizzle. A couple of cute young girls in tight pants and big hair manned clipboards and were asking passers-by to sign. It didn't take a genius to see it was some kind of petition and it didn't take a rocket scientist to guess who the instigator had been.

Another car's brakes screeched as they slammed to a halt behind her. Some forthright language ensued. Morgan made to turn left only to find the car park was full. She had to drive around the block and then some to find a parking space.

A good five minutes later she tied the black satin ribbon of her cashmere poncho tight around her neck, tugged her striped beanie down around her ears, shoved her large sunnies onto her nose and stormed onto Como Avenue having raised a good-sized head of steam.

The brass Bacio Bacio bell announced her arrival. She whipped off her sunnies and threw them into her oversized handbag in which that day's *Herald Sun* newspaper was rolled up ready to whack Saxon over the head the first moment she laid eyes on him.

'How can I help ya?' the girl behind the counter asked through a mouthful of chewing gum.

'Saxon?' Morgan said, not trusting more words than that would come out without spitting fire as well.

The girl shrugged. 'Dunno.'

'He's here somewhere.' Morgan knew it. It was as though he left a trail of ectoplasm on the air that only she could sense.

'Somewhere,' the girl agreed. 'Hey, you're Saxon's new girl, aren't ya?'

Morgan blinked. 'I'm…no. I'm not Saxon's new girl.' *I may have been an easy chump for a few moments in the car park the day before, but this morning's newspaper proves I am not Saxon's anything. I'm England to his Germany. Yes, even perhaps Pussy Galore to his James Bond. But not his girl.*

'Sure y'are,' the girl said. 'I saw you here the other day. And yesterday at Auntie Tina's party. *With* Saxon.'

'I wasn't *with* Saxon, *per se*. I had come to talk to him. About business.'

Trisha shook her head. Slowly.

'What?' Morgan said. 'Why are you doing that?'

Trisha grinned and she saw the family resemblance. One hundred per cent pure Ciantar charm. 'Saxon doesn't have girls come around. Not like Darius and Angelo. They have hundreds. Most of them complete tramps. But Saxon hasn't really, ever, hardly since…well, since the divorce, I guess.'

The divorce? Saxon was divorced? And hadn't really hardly ever had girls around since? Oh, this girl was just too good to be true.

Morgan stepped further into the shop, trying to ignore the scent of freshly ground coffee beans on the air. Trying to forget how fantastic the coffee here really was. She couldn't get used to it. Couldn't get attached to the place. Even though every coffee she'd had since Saxon's had been rubbish. He'd spoilt her for all others. Another reason she wanted to whack him.

'How long has it been? Since the divorce, I mean.'

Trisha fluffed a hand through her big brunette hair. 'Years, I guess. I was like a kid at the time so it all happened in whispers.'

Morgan didn't know whether she had been given a

new weapon in the fight against Saxon's charms, or whether this news was a clue that it was already too late for any of that.

'Sax thinks you're the cat's pyjamas,' Trisha said, leaning her hip against the bench and picking at her fingernails. 'He couldn't take his eyes off of you. And he's always been the cool one. Not like the rest of the drooling idiots I am embarrassed to call my family. It all kinda made me gag, to tell you the truth.'

Morgan swallowed. And not because she wanted to gag. She swallowed as her mouth suddenly began to water like crazy. She shook her head. It couldn't matter. Not after what he had done. She shoved her hand into her open bag, curling her fingers around the newspaper within so tight she knew they'd come away smudged. 'You really don't know where he is?' she asked.

Trisha gave her a blank stare. 'I don't keep tags on the guy.'

'Of course you don't. If you see him, tell him…' She paused. 'No. Forget it. Don't tell him anything.'

'Yeah, whatever.'

Morgan spun on her heel and headed into the laundry next door. The Changs greeted her with far more *bonhomie* than bored-to-her-eyeballs Trisha. And while Trisha had been too cool for school, she saw the very real strain behind the Changs' smiles.

'Miss Morgan,' Cassie said, coming out from behind the counter to take her by the hand as she bowed her hello. 'Have you come for a sausage?'

She shook her head. 'No, thanks, Mrs Chang.'

'They are very good. See how many people have come. How many of the locals love our stores. And want us to stay.'

Morgan dutifully looked out the smudged windows. Though she was pretty sure it had more to do with the free hot food on a cold winter's day than anything else. 'I'm looking for Saxon. Have you seen him?'

'Oh, yes,' said Cassie. 'It's because of him they do such good business next door. Ever since that horrible wife of his left. She was so bad for him. Bad for business.'

'She left him?' Morgan asked before she even felt the words forming. She wondered what had happened for any rational girl to leave such a guy. He was just so…everything. Beautiful, charming, funny, ambitious, a doer. And some kisser. Her stomach began to curdle at the mere memory. The backs of her knees followed suit, warming and melting, and she had to close her eyes to cut it off before it took hold of her completely. He was also a cad, she reminded herself as she squeezed the newspaper.

'Thank God,' Cassie said, crossing herself. 'It was his idea, you know. The signs and the sizzle. You should listen to him. He knows business. Even Mr Chang would agree. And Mr Chang believes he knows everything.'

'Right. Okay. I'll think about it.' Morgan extricated her hands from the older lady's and walked away. As she snuck past hordes of patrons she rubbed her cool hands together, trying to rid herself of the tinge of desperation she had felt in their grasp.

The delicious scent of pork sausages, white bread and tomato sauce wafted on the air. She hadn't had good coffee, nor had she had breakfast. The moment she'd opened up the newspaper left outside her hotel door she'd thought of little bar getting here and quick.

Now the combination of scents lit her insides with ravenous hunger. It was a combination that brought back happy memories of growing up in suburban Melbourne. Sitting on a garden chair in her parents' Richmond Hill home, watching her dad turn sausages on the barbecue, the scent of charred meat curling past her nose. And his smile. His loving smile that only grew tenfold whenever her mother was in sight. She swallowed down the remembrance and decided to breathe through her mouth.

She looked through the window of the Punjabi Palace. Unlike two days before, customers filled the tables. The Purans held court, but there was no sign of a tall, roguish dark haired man in amongst the crowd.

She swore beneath her breath and stalked through the crowd to the real-estate agent. She only went inside to escape the hordes and the evocative scents.

'Morgan,' Morris Cosgrove said as though he'd discovered a long-lost friend. He heaved his hulking form away from his desk and with his barrel chest puffed out waddled over to her. 'To what do I owe the pleasure? I have access to any number of nearby apartments and would be happy to—'

'Morris!' Spindly Adele strode out from the back room, tugging her aubergine suit jacket over her brown bengaline pants, while her beady gaze flickered over Morgan's black poncho, long-sleeved red Chloe T-shirt, and Sass and Bide jeans, lingering for a few seconds on her electric-blue boots. Morris froze, and seemed to shrink three sizes with one release of breath.

'Excuse my brother,' Adele said. 'He was trying to be funny. Instead he's usually just very trying.'

Morgan shook Adele's hand, but did spare an apologetic glance for Morris. Feeling as though it was her fault he was in trouble.

'*Are* you in the market for real estate?' Her squinty brown eyes lit bright. 'We can set you up with a nice apartment on this side of town. Of course, if you are going back to Paris, then…' Adele let her hopeful voice trail off.

Morgan swallowed down a great lump filling her throat. 'I was actually just looking for Saxon.'

Adele's small eyes suddenly swam with affection, and not a little lust. 'Oh,' she said, her reedy voice coming over husky. It seemed Saxon cast himself a wide spell. 'He is usually the one people around here come to see.'

'Have you seen him?' she asked, not falling for Adele's bait. She was looking for Saxon to yell at him, not to constantly be reminded that he was wonderful, or fabulous, or a lifesaver, or the hottest guy to ever walk the planet.

Adele ignored her question and said, 'You do so remind me of someone Saxon once knew.'

'Do I now?' Morgan said, digging her nails into her palms. She didn't need to ask who. It was like a recurrent theme of her morning.

'Adriana was a fashion plate too. Dripping in labels. Wouldn't be seen dead with any of us. Almost sent Saxon broke on the cost of her haircuts alone. You don't look all that much like her, though. She was tall, dark, glamorous. Big boobs, big teeth, drop-dead gorgeous. Italian. A walking nightmare, basically.' Adele lifted her chin and glared down her thin nose at Morgan. 'I knew it would never last.'

Adriana. He'd been married to a drop-dead gorgeous someone called Adriana. With shiny hair and fancy taste. Morgan was small, on the skinny side, had messy hair, and liked free designer stuff mostly because it was free. She wasn't sure how that made her similar, but she wondered if Saxon saw her the same way. If that was why he was taken with her. Or if that was why he was busy stabbing her in the back every chance he got.

She tugged her beanie tighter around her ears, as though it was some kind of protection. And she used the look in Adele's eyes as a wake-up call. She had no intention of being one of the guy's satellites. One of his band of lonely women hanging off his every word, dreaming of his large hands and warm, melting kisses, needing to make up excuses to see him. Which was *not* what she was doing there at all.

Even if Trisha was right and he did in fact think her the cat's pyjamas, it didn't matter. Her father had thought of her mother in that way, and the moment he was gone she had simply washed her hands of him and married someone else. His best friend, no less.

Morgan had learnt early on that you simply couldn't trust blind hope. You couldn't rely on a love that lasted a lifetime. Someone always loved someone else more, meaning that other someone would just end up getting hurt. She was coming to realise that Saxon Ciantar was just a whole world of hurt wrapped up in pretty packaging.

'It's hard not to like old Saxon,' Morris suddenly piped up from his desk where he was now eating a cold hotdog. 'Especially after seeing how he has turned his business around since the vamp did a runner. It kinda terrifies me what might happen to the rest of us if we're not bundled in under his umbrella. But then if we go belly up I could always take that trip to the Gold Coast. Sunshine would be nice right now.'

Adele's eyes turned cool, but she didn't even need to turn for Morris to obviously feel it. He ducked his head.

'Do you know where he is?' Morgan asked, deciding it best not to get in the middle of them.

Adele crossed her arms across her flat chest, and glared. 'Nope. No idea.'

Morgan didn't believe her for a second. She leant sideways to look over Adele's shoulder. 'Morris, any idea?'

'He was in here about five minutes ago. I think he was heading in to see Jan.'

Morgan let out a long-held breath. 'Great. Thanks, Morris.' She gave them both a quick nod before leaving with the wind at her heels.

He was near. She could feel it. Her legs were a little shakier. Her heart rate a little faster. And she was finding it harder to breathe normally.

Her hand dived into her handbag, gripped onto the newspaper and readied herself to slap him over the back of the head with it when she finally had him cornered.

If she found herself bending, wilting, keening towards him, she could always knock herself out instead.

CHAPTER SIX

SAXON sipped on a cup of terrible tea from Jan's mismatched china, then placed it back onto the wicker coffee-table in the tiny back room of her shop.

'So how are you getting along with our new landlord?' Jan asked, settling into a plush lounge chair, a puff of dust lifting off the arms and slowly settling back from whence it came.

'We are getting along as good as can be expected. For two people at complete odds. So far she hasn't thrown anything heavy at me and I have restrained from trying to have her deported. I'm actually quite proud of the both of us.'

'I can't help but like her myself,' Jan said. 'There is something of the wounded bird about her that I found instantly endearing.'

'How wounded, do you think?' he asked.

Jan's knowing smile grew, and he cursed himself, and the strange tea, and the warm, dark, comforting room. Jan shrugged. 'I'm not sure it's my place to find out.'

Meaning it was his. There was no point denying it with Jan. If one day he discovered she was three hundred years old and some kind of good witch he wouldn't be surprised.

Saxon played with the medallion hanging around his neck. 'I'm not sure that I *want* to find out. Might make it more difficult to go about the business of systematically pulling the rug out from under her.'

Jan said nothing. She just blinked wise eyes and waited for him to figure it out.

'This is big business, Jan. And small business. And our business. This place may be a symbol of my family's resilience, but it's your very livelihood. I don't think we can refer to our consciences all that many times before it makes us too weak to fight back.'

Jan leaned forward, her chandelier-shaped earrings chiming prettily. Hypnotically. 'There is an ebb and a flow to life. None of us can hang on so tight that we don't get caught up in the waves at least a little, or we will simply be worn away by time.'

'Tell that to the Changs, the Purans, and the Cosgroves.'

Jan smiled. 'Don't think I won't. Now, what kind of bird will our new little friend turn out to be, do you think? A chicken who will fly back to her coop? Or a phoenix set to rise from our ashes?'

'Shall we start a betting pool?' Saxon asked.

His honest answer was he truly hoped she would turn out to be neither. More and more, every day, he strove to come up with a way to satisfy all parties. But every day he found a new way to steamroll her, he was less and less sure that could ever happen. Something and somebody would have to give. And if it turned out to be him, he'd never forgive himself. Fool him twice…

'Jan?' a female voice called out from the shop.

Saxon held out a hand to stop her from calling back. Even from that one small word he knew her voice. The timbre, the volume, the exact note.

'She's not really here looking for me,' Jan said. 'Shall I send her in here and give you two some privacy or kick her out on her ear?'

Saxon's laugh was wretched. Jan patted him on the knee.

'Coming, Morgan!' she said, closing the purple and gold velveteen curtains so that nobody would know he was there.

Morgan played with the corner of a damask cushion, letting the weave tickle against her palm as she waited.

She just loved this shop. It was filled with secrets and treasures. She could have spent a week poring through the reams of fabric stacked to the rafters in great, teetering, seemingly random piles, trawling through boxes of beads and coloured cord, and cataloguing the most amazing range of wools.

Morgan heard a strange noise from somewhere in the back of the shop—it sounded like something between a cough and a laugh. She glared into the darkness but heard nothing more. Then Jan seemed to appear from nowhere, and Morgan stopped touching things, and dreaming.

'Good morning, darling,' Jan said, leaning in and kissing her on the cheek. She smelled of chamomile tea and mothballs. 'What can I help you with this fine day? Have you decided to take home the Battenberg lace after all?'

Morgan's gaze shot straight to the folded pile of white lace tucked in between a dozen others, surprised that Jan had remembered how taken with it she had been two days before. 'Ah, no. Though that isn't a firm no, I can assure you. Maybe when I have more time.'

'Here.' Jan reached up and cut off a short strip, just enough for a collar, or a couple of cuffs, or a rosette for the poncho she now wore. Just enough to whet her appetite. A taste test, as it were. And the moment she touched the fabric, and saw the out-of–this-world detail up close, she knew she'd be back for more.

'Now if you didn't come for the lace,' Jan said, 'or the sausage sizzle, I assume you are here for our man Saxon.'

'I am,' she said. 'But, please, don't spend the next five minutes telling me how wonderful and fabulous and gorgeous he is. I've heard enough for one day. Just, please, if you know where he might be, point the way.'

'You don't think him wonderful or fabulous, I take it,' Jan said, moving over to the cash register towards the back of the shop and picking up a book. Morgan could only guess it was an address book, so she followed.

'Not today.' Morgan pulled out the offending news-paper, flapping it open to the fifth page. 'Did you know about this?'

Jan glanced down at it. 'No. I don't read the news-paper. Or watch the news. Or those awful current affairs shows. They always make everything seem so grim.'

'Tell me about it. Your hero has managed to plant a story in here about me. I come across as some kind of Goliath. I'm five foot six, in heels! While he, and all his big and tallness, comes across as some local David. While at the same time highlighting the fact that he has eighteen classic cars and a private family jet.'

When he'd offered to take her to the Opera in Sydney she'd never once imagined it would be in his own plane.

'All's fair in love and war, don't they say?' Jan asked.

Morgan ignored the obvious gist behind that comment and rolled up her newspaper again into the perfect shape with which to beat him up when she finally found the guy.

'So, is that why you don't think him wonderful and fabulous?' Jan asked. 'Because he's wily? I would think one does not end up with eighteen classic cars without being somewhat shrewd.'

Morgan lifted her chin. 'I don't know him well enough to even begin to think one way or the other.'

'But you liked me instantly,' Jan said, putting the book down and reaching out for another. 'Just as I liked you instantly. Just as you thought the Changs kind, the Purans shy, and the Cosgroves complicated. You no doubt had an instant reaction to Saxon as well.'

'Well, sure. I guess that's true.'

Jan looked up with a smile. An encouraging smile that said, *Tell me, and then I'll tell you where you'll find him.* Compromise. This whole darned endeavour was all about compromise. Something she'd never been any good at.

She swallowed down the desire to turn and walk away, knowing that as always the only way forward was in truth. The truth couldn't offend. It was black and white. Freedom on the other hand had always seemed to her the pristine, perfect, dreamy blue of open waters and clear skies. Beauty was all the colours of autumn. While the colour she had *instantly* associated with Saxon Ciantar had been heartbreak red, and not one thing he'd done had changed her mind.

'I thought him…arrogant,' she admitted. 'Scruffy. And somewhat full of himself.'

Again Morgan heard the coughing laughing sound; she looked through the stacks of treasures hoping to discover a Saxon-sized shape in the gloom. 'Do you have a cat?'

'Oh, no,' Jan said, slamming the book shut so hard Morgan's gaze sprang back to hers. 'I'm allergic. And now? Do you still think him arrogant, scruffy, and full of himself?'

Morgan remembered him the second time they'd met, with the gorgeous suit in her hotel bar. Then comfortable in his skin at the family party. And far less dressed in the insanely erotic escapades that had invaded her dreams night after night.

'Scruffy? Not so much. Arrogant. God, yes. Full of himself? If what I've heard today from the others in the strip were to be believed, then no. Perhaps not as much as he seems.'

'Or perhaps he has good reason to be sure of himself,' Jan said with a purely feminine smile.

Morgan bit her lip, but that didn't hide her smile. 'Fine. I admit it; he has plenty of reason to think himself God's gift to women. He's too good-looking for comfort. He's ridiculously successful. And he has charm oozing out of every pore.'

'Sounds like you've thought more about this than perhaps you were letting on before.'

'More than I wish I had,' she mumbled. 'Now that you've forced that out of me, Jan, please, return the favour, and tell me where Super Saxon is. He knows I'm here. I know he knows. If he's such a hero why is he hiding?'

Jan's smile widened. 'Did you check if his car is

out back? Wherever you find that pile of old metal you'll find him.'

Morgan clicked her tongue against her cheek. 'Of course. Ta.' She backed away, sparing one last glance at the dark corners at the back of the shop.

'Good luck,' Jan called out.

Morgan gave her a wave, wondering for a moment if she meant with finding Saxon, or with something else entirely.

'You still here?' Jan asked, as she drifted into the back room.

'Of course I am,' Saxon said. 'You made it far too interesting for me to leave.'

'Did I give you any of the answers you were looking for?'

'No. Maybe.' He stood and ran a hand over his chin. 'I don't know. She's gone?'

Jan nodded. 'If you hurry you can still catch her.'

Saxon leaned in and gave Jan a quick kiss on the cheek. 'One of these days your meddling is going to get you into trouble.'

'But not today,' she said.

And just before he slipped out the back door, Jan said. 'Super Saxon? Does that come with supersonic hearing? Or can you see through walls?'

'I'll never tell,' he said, before shutting the door, and turning a fast walk into a jog into a flat-out run.

Once Saxon had started Bessie, he gave her a couple of minutes to warm up. But he was also giving Morgan time to walk through the crowds and around the back of Bacio Bacio to find him.

He turned the dial on the old stereo until he found a jazz station playing Ella Fitzgerald, then closed his eyes, leant back against the leather headrest, and waited.

A *rap rap rap* on the driver's side window knocked him from his reverie. He opened one eye to find Morgan: lips pursed, arms crossed. Though he couldn't tell if she was glaring at him from behind her large sunglasses, he had no doubt that was what she was trying to do.

Today her hair was in two pigtails, covered with a multicoloured beanie with two pom-poms hanging off ropes dangling from the ends of the ear covers. She looked angry, but so very cute.

Saxon wound down the window using the manual handle. 'Good morning,' he said with a big friendly grin. 'This is a pleasant surprise.'

'What's this?' she asked, waving a hunk of newspaper at him and expending with any niceties.

He didn't need a closer look to know what it was. He'd called a friend at the *Herald Sun* the minute she'd walked out his door that first day. When he'd seen the article that morning he'd actually winced. But he still said, 'Um, how many guesses do I get?'

'It's the ridiculous article you no doubt spoonfed to some lazy journalist.'

'So no guesses, then.'

'Saxon!'

'Morgan!' he shot back using her same tone. Then he waved his hand towards her sunglasses. 'Big night? Or just couldn't sleep?'

Her cheeks turned pink, glorious, healthy, glowing pink. She whipped off her sunglasses and all but threw them into her big handbag. Once again her beautiful green eyes took his breath away. They were fiery, and sparkling. God, but she was something out of the box.

'You can't do this!' she said. 'You can't go around planting stories and bribing people to sign petitions and using serious bodies such as the Heritage Council for your own measly ends.'

He leant his arm along the edge of the window and let all that beautiful energy wash over him. 'And why not?'

'Because there is no historical or community value inherent in one single brick. I've been here three days running and the first two I was the only shopper in sight and I didn't spend a cent.'

'Of course you didn't. Them's the perks of owning such a friendly place.'

'Saxon, you're only delaying the inevitable. Why don't you stop mucking about and let what's going to happen anyway just happen?'

Saxon didn't have a comeback for that one. Especially since she'd pretty much voiced what Jan had tried to tell him, though in far less mystical terms. But he'd deal with all that later.

Right now, if *she* wasn't careful, what was going to happen was that he was going to reach out and tuck his hand behind her neck and draw her to him and kiss her. He wondered if she would stop mucking about and let that happen. All things considering he thought it a fifty per cent chance all that hostility would slip into sexual energy without even a hiccup and she would climb through the window to get to him. And a fifty per cent chance she'd slap him with the newspaper. Okay, eighty per cent chance.

Saxon regretfully put the dampers on his attraction. 'I guess that's up to the council, then, isn't it?'

'Thank God for small mercies.'

Her mouth creased into a malevolent grin and Saxon wondered for a moment if he was creating a monster. Pity that he was having far too much fun watching this one spit fire. Despite the pom-poms, and the pink nose from standing in the blistering cold for too long, he had already come to the conclusion she was quite simply the sexiest woman he had ever met. His mother's insistence she needed more pasta in her diet aside, it had been some time since he'd decided he wouldn't change one single thing about her. Well, apart from the fact that she wouldn't realise he knew best and do as she was told.

She continued glaring at him, waiting for him to make the next move. He did. He smiled pleasantly and said, 'Well, good luck with all that, then. I'm off, so *ciao* for now!'

He gunned the engine and looked over his shoulder to make sure nobody was in the way of his car. Though he had no intention of driving away. He had every intention of pushing her buttons for a good while yet.

When he looked back to the front, she had disappeared. That was all he was going to get from her today? He felt let down. Ready even to turn Bessie off and chase her. Casually, so she wouldn't realise that was what he was doing.

Was that what he had been doing all along? Chasing her? A woman with the heart of his family business in her hands. A woman who preferred cool, cosmopolitan Paris to the sheer relaxed perfection of Melbourne, and designer clothes and cocktails to beer and pizza. Well, he certainly had a type…

That dulling thought was almost enough to have him

gun the engine for real and leave, to put some distance, mental and physical, between him and the woman at the forefront of his every thought.

But then suddenly his passenger door was wrenched open and she was inside his car, buckling herself in.

Again the heater made the most of her subtle cherry scent. He wondered if he managed to find the exact place she dabbed her perfume, whether it would taste as good as it smelled. And if he didn't have a gelato in stores in that exact flavour before summer he didn't deserve to be in charge of a multimillion-dollar business.

'Somewhere you want me to take you?' he asked.

His arm still rested along the back of her seat. His fingers were so close to her hair it pained him not reaching out and playing with her pigtail, letting all that softness slide against his fingers. He convinced himself to hold back. And not because of any fear that he was becoming too enamoured too fast; it was far too late for all that. He held back as he knew he would get his chance later. It was all about timing.

'Not at all,' she said, shooting him a frosty glare. 'I have a rental for the rest of the week. But don't let me stop you. You go wherever it is you need to go, and while you drive you can listen to me talk.'

'You don't want to know where I am heading?'

She shook her head and crossed her arms. 'All I care about is making you understand that if you push me one more inch, I will not give you or your cronies any more chances to convince me that I can make this place work as is. I will start plans to redevelop. And I will sell out to some nasty conglomerate in nine years' time with absolutely no input from any of you.'

And though that didn't sound like the most fun conversation he'd ever had, Saxon realised he was willing to listen to a great deal of such hot air to have this woman sitting in his car. To have her close enough to touch. To bathe in her black-cherry scent. To imagine exactly how and when he would get the chance to kiss her again. Because by the end of this day he *would* kiss her.

He unwrapped a stick of cinnamon gum, popped it into his mouth, looked over his shoulder as he finally backed down the cracked concrete driveway. 'Get comfortable, then. This is going to be some ride.'

'Now get a load of this part.' Morgan flapped the paper straight and quoted.

'Ciantar, with his sixty shopfronts, multi-faceted stock portfolio, private plane, eighteen classic cars stored in a private garage in the family winery, and his millions upon millions behind him...'

She let the paper drop. The very numbers made her feel a little faint. 'I have no idea how you can possibly come across as sympathetic with that kind of backing. If this dodgy mate of yours was actually any kind of decent journo he could have come to me for a copy of my assets and bank balance that would have changed the tone of your article here no end: Kipling-Rossetti with her maxed out VisaCard, small collection of vintage purses and down-payment on a worsted sofa...'

Saxon laughed. 'What are you really trying to say, Morgan? That prosperous people are by their nature always the baddies?'

'No, I wasn't saying that. But now you mention it…'

She glanced across to find he was still smiling as he hummed along with some jazz number on the car stereo. The window was open, just a smidge, but enough to let a stream of winter air into the car. It mussed his dark hair, sending it flickering away from his high forehead. His eyes squinted against the bright winter sun, but he didn't bother with sunglasses.

She felt a sudden kick of sadness that she couldn't just sit back and enjoy riding in this great car with this gorgeous man at her side. That life couldn't give her a break and suddenly make him Parisian. And compliant. And mute.

'You don't endear me to your cause when you keep sabotaging me, Saxon. And for what? A drop in the ocean compared with what you are really worth. Why don't you set up a meeting with the rest of your family? I'm sure I can make them see sense. Even if you can't.'

'Ain't gonna happen. If you think I'm being hard-headed now, bring my family into this and you'll not know what has hit you.' He spared her a quick glance and by the look in his eyes she knew she wasn't getting through to him. Not one little bit. Not even by chip-chip-chipping away for the past hour. Or was it two?

Oh, what the hell? She was losing her voice anyway. The conversation came to a comfortable lull and she let it. With a strangely contented sigh Morgan rested her left elbow on the window sill and simply watched the world whip by.

'At what point did trams and smog give way to small town cafés and truck stops?' she asked.

Saxon pulled the car to the side of the road. He held

out a finger and, for fear it might land upon her mouth again, she snapped her lips shut tight.

'I'll be back in a sec',' he said, before dragging his long legs out of the car with the grace of a guy half his size.

More signs caught Morgan's attention. '"Snowboard hire. Toboggans. Convenient On Mountain Service,"' she read out. 'Where the hell are we?'

Saxon and another guy came out of a shop carrying great hulking chains.

Morgan looked for the button to wind down the window. It took her far longer than it ought to have to realise that was what the handle on the door was for. It took both hands to get the old metal to wind far enough. 'Saxon,' she called out.

'Won't be long,' he said from somewhere near the back of the car. She looked in the rear-vision mirror but he was gone again. A few seconds later Saxon appeared beside the door. He patted the guy on the back and waved before hopping back into the car. His nose was pink, and he'd brought the winter cold inside with him. Morgan ran her hands up and down her arms. Saxon noticed and thoughtfully turned up the heat.

'Where are you going, exactly?' she asked.

Saxon's smile grew. And she suddenly wasn't comfortable any more. She'd been crazy to think she could be in this guy's company. That smile was built to turn female knees to putty. Her heart thumped against her ribs. Her veins thrummed. It was kind of scary how much this person could affect her with a simple movement of facial muscles.

'I thought you'd never ask,' he said. 'Now don't get too excited, but we are spending the night on Mount Buller.'

She blinked. She turned to face the side window so fast she almost got whiplash. As they gathered speed and began to climb her hearing turned fuzzy. The trees whipping past were taller, thinner. Alpine green. The air sliding through the gap in Saxon's window was colder. And through a gap in the dense forest to her left she saw a distant snow-capped mountain.

'Mount Buller,' she repeated slowly as her geography came back to her. 'You're going to the *snow*?'

'No, *we're* going to the snow,' he said as though it were some great surprise gift.

'Are you completely mad?'

'Not at all. My bag's in the back if you don't believe me. You just happened to jump in my car and insist I take you with me, which was a nice turn of events. The snow is the kind of place where it's always better if one has company. Much warmer that way.'

Morgan's mouth dropped open and she couldn't even hope to think of a comeback.

'Just think,' he said, as though he were completely unaware she was turning pink with rage beside him, 'this way you can keep an eye on me all night. Make sure I'm not up to any more no good. I'll let you listen in on every phone call I make. I won't leave your sight for one second. And I'll even buy you that steak dinner I promised. You can't lose.'

She couldn't lose? There was plenty she could lose while alone with this guy at the snow. The shirt off her back being the least of it.

She had her big handbag, at least. And her wallet. She could find a bus back to Melbourne, though they would likely all be fully booked this time of year. Or she could insist on finding her own accommodation, though her credit card was maxed out already after this impromptu trip to Melbourne. At least she had the rolled-up newspaper, which she could still use to knock him over the head if he tried anything. If he touched her, or kissed her, or looked at her that way that made her every reservation fade into oblivion.

Her ears finally popped as they scooted up the incline, passing under the 'Welcome to Mt Buller' sign. Saxon flashed his membership card before heading up the shiny black bitumen slope, wet with melted snow.

At the visitors' car park they had to leave Bessie and take a bus up to the Alpine Village. Morgan looked wistfully through the back window hoping to think of some brilliant way to get herself out of this mess. Especially since Saxon was crammed in beside her, all big and warm and smelling of cinnamon. Surrounded by all this snow there was no way she should have felt anywhere near as hot.

Saxon leant across and pointed out the window. 'Most of the trees hidden beneath those great fat mounds of snow are snow gums. And the skinny ones leaning over the pathways are wooly buts.'

Morgan closed her eyes and breathed through her mouth. 'I know.' She opened her eyes again to find him watching her with that one sexily raised eyebrow.

'Been here before have we?'

Morgan nodded.

'Did your family ski?'

She considered giving him the silent treatment until they got back to Melbourne. But that would only give him more time to talk. To pry. To provoke. To whisper sweet nothings. 'My mother,' she said through gritted teeth, 'skied.'

Her mother who had given her a white ski outfit for her third birthday. Until her father had pointed out she would get lost on the slopes in such an ensemble. Her mother had sulked, while her father had been the one to dress her in a brand-new red outfit the next day. That pretty much summed up her childhood. Her father loved. Her mother skied.

'Past tense?'

'I wouldn't know. I haven't spoken to her in several years.'

'Since Paris?' he asked, his face giving away nothing.

'Around about that time.'

'You haven't considered catching up while you're here?'

'That's right,' she said. 'I haven't.'

She waited for him to raise the other eyebrow or cross himself in shock that her family was not as bounteous and inclusive as his own. But his gorgeous brown eyes looked deep into hers, making all the last parts of her that were bitten by the cold simply melt into a pool of warmth. And then he said, 'All the more time to spend with me, then.'

His words were kind but his eyes were kinder still, and Morgan felt a strange stinging sensation behind her eyes. The stinging amplified when he reached across and took her hand in his.

Who was she kidding? She *ached* for him to touch her, and kiss her, or look at her that way that made her every reservation fade into oblivion. She wanted all that and more. She wanted everything.

The small bus chugged to a halt once. Morgan spilled out onto the snow-swept path and took several steps clear until she felt as if she could breathe again. She looked around to get her bearings as she hadn't been at the snow since she was a pre-schooler.

Of course it was beautiful. Picture-postcard pretty. Romantic as all get out. Chalets and hotels with A-line rooves in lovely shades of yellow and red and brown were covered in a blanket of snow. Skiers in a multitude of coloured outfits covered the main slope in a slash of skis, and a dash of snowboards beneath the great grey skeletal monster that was the ever-revolving ski-lift.

'This way,' Saxon said, lugging a great caramel leather bag over his shoulder and leading her into the village proper.

Even at his side she soon grew cold. Freezing cold. She was way underdressed. Everyone they passed wore bulky thermals and ski boots and parkas and gloves and scarves. She wore a beanie with pom-poms, a cashmere poncho and electric blue stiletto-heeled boots. She felt their eyes travel over her get-up as if she had landed there from another planet. She told herself they wouldn't know a red Chloe T-shirt if it turned their white shirts pink in the wash, but it didn't much help her plummeting confidence.

'Everyone is staring at me,' she said.

Saxon put his arm around her waist and leaned in to whisper, 'They're staring because you're adorable.'

'They're staring because I look ridiculous.'

'You looked exactly the same in Carlton. Did they stare at you there?'

'No.'

'Actually they did. When you were leaning in my car I saw at least three guys walk past and stare at you. The fact that you were so kindly giving them an excellent view of your sweet rear end may have helped there.'

'I don't fit in here, Saxon,' she said, huddling in closer. *Dad and I never did.*

'Fit in where exactly?' he asked, his voice rich with laughter.

'In the land of money, and privilege, and snow people. I can't ski. I hate the cold. And I've always been too small that I get lost inside those puffy jackets.'

He pulled her closer to help her avoid bumping into a foursome of snow people in multicoloured beanies with goggles atop their heads shuffling along the snowy path wearing what looked like tennis racquets on their feet.

Why they all insisted on wearing mismatched clothes and clashing colours she had no idea. It was as if they were in some kind of cult, and she'd never been given the password. There were people who loved the snow and those who just didn't get it. She was definitely one of the latter.

Saxon grabbed her hand and led her up a set of metallic grey steps. The snow all around made the world suddenly seem monochromatic. Cold. Austere. Against the white and grey backdrop Saxon, with his chocolate-brown hair, olive skin, and deep brown eyes, looked like pure warmth. Familiarity. Comfort. Vigour. All things bright and beautiful.

He helped her up the last of the slippery steps. As he pulled her against him the breath left her lungs in a great whoosh. He tucked her hand into the crook of his arm and smiled down into her eyes and her heart did a slow backward roll until she felt inside out and back to front. If this guy turned out to be one of the former, filthy rich *and* a snow person, she might as well just throw in the towel right now.

'Come on, sunshine,' he said, his voice so low it didn't carry any further than her cold ears, 'not far to go now.'

He wrapped an arm about her, folding her inside his leather jacket, holding her close. It came to her, slow and warm, like a hot drink warming her hands on a cold day, what a beautiful man he was. He was stubborn and antagonistic and smooth as the froth that topped his fantabulous lattes. But he was also kind, and sincere, and generous. And beautiful. Physically, truly beautiful.

She fought against the sudden urge to slide her hands along his flat stomach, beneath his shirt until she found skin. Warm, smooth, masculine, beautiful skin. She wanted to touch, caress, scrape the ridges of his muscles with the backs of her fingernails until his eyes turned as dark as midnight.

She looked down at her feet, mostly so that Saxon could not see the hit of pure unadulterated, sexual attraction building in her eyes.

'Are you here for a reason?' she asked, desperate to get her mind off the subject of Saxon and sex. The fact that he was pressed snugly up against the edge of her left breast didn't help one little bit. 'Do you have a shop up here?'

'Nope. I just come up here for some R and R a few weekends every winter. To tell you the truth none of the rest of my family can stand the snow so it's the one place I can truly get away.'

'So you don't have meetings or plans as such?'

He smiled as though he knew exactly what she was asking. 'Sorry, Morgan, for the next twenty-four hours I'm all yours.'

All hers. For twenty-four hours. Miles from any-where. From Melbourne, or Paris, or her hotel phone. Miles from the shop, or the other tenants with their beseeching eyes and wringing hands.

Just her, and him, and acres of pristine white snow.

CHAPTER SEVEN

'HERE we are,' Saxon said, leading Morgan up to the front door of a three-storey lodge made of pale grey brick and white shingles.

He had to let go of her to find the key to the front door, and she realised again how cold it truly was when he wasn't there to hold her close. She wasn't used to this kind of need, this kind of hollow left behind when a particular person wasn't there. She didn't quite know what it meant; only that she felt as if she was waiting for the other shoe to drop.

'Come on in,' Saxon said, scraping the snow off the bottom of his boots before heading inside.

Morgan gingerly followed him into a large open-plan lounge room with fat wooden beams cutting across a twenty-foot canted ceiling, a rustic brick fireplace filled with fresh logs, and overstuffed cream couches with red and dark brown rugs thrown haphazardly over the back of each.

Saxon slid off his boots, and left them on a mat at the front door. Morgan bent down to unzip her own boots, though she paused when the look of the dark grey slate floor made her toes curl.

'We have underfloor heating,' Saxon said. 'I called and had it turned on when we hit Mirrimbah. It'll be warmer than your socks.'

'Right.' She still shivered slightly as her feet hit soft temperate tile.

Saxon threw his bag, and then his leather jacket, onto a low rustic bench against the wall and went about turning on lamps, which threw patches of golden light around the room.

Morgan was drawn to a wide cushion-covered window-seat. Through the uncovered glass fresh powder had turned the whole world pure white. Skinny, silver-barked trees grew at forty-five-degree angles to combat the heavy weight of snow. And through the criss-cross of branches and trunks, slashing rays of sun lit the ground all the way to the summit.

'And that's only the beginning,' Saxon said from just behind her.

Morgan spun to find him watching her with a small smile on his face. In a sky-blue T-shirt and jeans he looked so edible, she had to swallow. 'The beginning of what?'

'The beauty of this place.'

She blinked, not quite sure if he meant natural beauty, or the beauty of being holed up here with the likes of him. 'Who do I ask to get my own room?'

'Me,' he said, crossing his arms across his burly chest. 'I own the lodge. There are five bedrooms and four bathrooms, though usually when I come to stay I come alone. And I only use the one room.'

She followed the direction of his gaze and through an open doorway saw a large rustic bed covered in a much-washed multicoloured patchwork quilt.

'So what do you want to do first?' he asked. Her gaze swung back to him to find his eyes were dark and gleaming. 'Lunch? Slope time? A grand tour of my humble abode?'

His question was clear. Go back out there where she would have to travel the slippery terrain in her high-heeled boots and put up with disconcerting stares from the locals. Where the chances were high she might bump into someone her mother knew.

Or stay. Here. Alone. With him.

Lit by the bright winter sun beaming through the nearby window his eyes were crystal-clear. His smile provocative. His skin smooth, but lived-in. His shoulders broad and sturdy. He was everything she was not. He was confident, easygoing, and unflappable, while she felt as if she were holding onto the life she'd chosen by ragged fingernails. While he celebrated his life with passion, and noise and gusto she was so uptight she feared one day she might simply implode. Yet of all the women in all the world he could have kidnapped to his cabin in the snow, he'd picked her.

She took a step his way, coerced by barefaced attraction, inescapable compulsion, and a need to have the essence of this man wash over her, infuse her, and transform her.

'How about I let you decide?' she said, hardly recognising her own voice. 'When you turned the car in this direction and kidnapped me away from the city, you must have had some kind of plan for what would happen when we got here.'

'I brought you here,' he said, his voice husky, deep and slow, 'against your will, because I have wanted to be alone with you from the moment I laid eyes on you.'

Then he swallowed. Barely. Just the rise and fall of his throat. But it was enough for her to know he wasn't any cooler about what was happening between them than she was.

She tilted so that she could look straight into his eyes. 'So now you have me here what are you going to do with me?'

'This,' he said, his deep voice creating curls of heat in her stomach. He peeled her hand away from her side and slowly bent it behind her back until she was flush against him. The evidence that he wanted her was rock-hard against her stomach. Then with his spare hand he slowly pulled her beanie off her head. The knitted wool tugged at her hair, the static making it flyaway and messy. She lifted her hand to run it over her hair.

'Uh-uh,' he said. And her hand fluttered back to her side. He took it too and bent it behind her also, then pressed her against the back of the couch, trapping her hands behind her back. She was not only kidnapped, now she was to all intents and purposes bound. Her breath wavered from her lungs as she began to tremble.

She ached to let her eyes drift closed, to simply enjoy the feelings rocketing from the tip of her head to the bottom of her bare feet. But that would have meant missing out on the view. The rich brown hair pushed off his face by tracks of his fingers. Dark eyes so full of se-ductive self-belief. The shadow of stubble across his jaw making him seem just wicked enough to play this game.

The impulse to protect herself clamoured to the surface, to make him think this was all in a day's play. That this wasn't special. Unique. Exotic. The sexiest she had ever felt in her whole entire life. If he saw that, if he knew that, then he would know…everything.

'Is that it?' she asked, blinking coquettishly.

His forehead split into a questioning frown.

'If I remember rightly I was at one stage promised the best I ever had.'

Saxon laughed, the rich throaty sound skittering across her tightly strung nerves. 'Way to put pressure on a guy,' he said.

She gathered every ounce of strength she had and rose up to press herself against him. She locked her hands together behind her still, her fingernails biting into her palms. She itched to rasp her fingers over his chin, through his hair, but it was more erotic to deny herself just a little longer. 'Are you telling me that you're recanting?'

Saxon breathed out through his nose. He then slowly let his hands drop to rest gently at her throat, his thumbs curved into the sensitive dip at the base of her neck. His gaze dropped to her parted lips. His tongue darted out to wet his own lips and her chest constricted. His mouth tipped into a smile. A smile that told her he knew exactly what he was doing to her.

Finally he looked back into her eyes and said, 'Not on your life, honey.'

And Morgan was glad the sofa was at her back as her knees gave way completely.

Her relief was short-lived as Saxon's admittedly lapse will-power gave way first. He slid his arms around her waist and pulled her close. She swayed to him like a rag doll, and before she knew it his mouth was on hers. She gave in and wrapped her arms around him. Pressing herself against him. Her out-of-control body needing to get closer, be closer.

The pleasure of his touch, his kiss, was already too

much to bear and they had only just begun. Some unnamed, unknown emotion welled fast and furious within her, tipping everything topsy-turvy. Her sense of self-preservation, and her sense in general, flipped over on itself until it was lost within the rowdy heat of desire filling her body until she ached. How would she ever survive this?

She ran her hands up his back, paying blissful attention as his muscles contracted beneath her touch. The soft cotton of his T-shirt was suddenly a great impediment. With one forceful tug she pulled his T-shirt from his jeans and let her hands rove beneath, the sensation of hot male flesh against the palms of her hands breathtaking.

But she needed more. Now. In a burst of need she ripped his shirt over his head. Unfortunately that meant that their lips had to part.

With barely a pause he kissed her cheek, her earlobe, and the hollow at the base of her neck, which she had never known could be such an erogenous zone until this man had made it so. Her mouth ached from not meshing with his to the point where she even might have whimpered. She wasn't all that sure for she couldn't hear anything much over the thrumming of blood in her head.

She was fast losing all sense of herself completely within his embrace. She opened her eyes to get her bearings, but all she could see was a pinpoint of light somewhere far away as if she were falling to the bottom of the ocean.

'Saxon,' she whispered, meaning for it to be a caution, but it sounded a heck of a lot more like an endearment.

'My God, Morgan,' he murmured, his mouth slipping past her ear, his hot breath making her shiver so hard she clung to him all the more. Then she captured his wandering mouth with hers and kissed him until no more words could form in her misty brain.

He gathered her tighter in his arms and tipped her back so that their kiss could grow. Intensify. Ripen. Until everything within her seemed to swell.

Her right leg wrapped around him, the scrape of denim against denim quaking through her. He captured her leg beneath the knee and pulled it high. Her hands dived into the long hair at the base of his neck, tugging and pulling and trailing her fingers beneath his soft, sexy mane.

With a growl that sent a shaft of heat straight through her centre he let her leg go so that he could grab her buttocks and lift her into his arms. She stole her legs around his hips, locking her ankles. She wrapped her arms around his neck and pressed her breasts against his naked chest.

There were far, far too many layers of cloth between her skin and his. Disappointment and frustration spread through her like a virus. 'Put me down,' she said, her voice ragged and all but unrecognisable.

'Ain't gonna happen,' he said, hefting her higher, closer, until she could feel the length of him cradled between her thighs. Hot, hard and ready. Her head tipped backwards as she gulped in much-needed air.

When she found the strength to pull her head upright once more, she looked right into his eyes. So dark. And infinitely deep. And completely enraptured by her. *Her.* Somehow she wasn't completely terrified by all that blatant need. Because she trusted him.

To do what? Take her to heaven? Treat her right? Never hurt her? She shook her messy, tumbling hair away from her face and shook herself free of those insidious thoughts. This wasn't about trust. This was about getting his naked skin on hers.

Her breath caught on every second word as she said, 'Unless you have an extra arm hidden somewhere on your person with which to disrobe me, you're going to have to let me down.'

Saxon bumped her backside against the back of the sofa. Instinctively she let go of him, her feet hit the floor and her hands grabbed hold of the sofa.

Before she even had her balance, his fingers unhooked the ribbon of her poncho. He didn't even wait for it to fall off her shoulders before he began tugging at the collar of her red T-shirt with his teeth, breathing hot air on the peak of her bra until she ached to rip her clothes from skin that felt as if it were on fire.

She arched into him as he travelled down her stomach, his teeth catching on cotton, the second-hand sensation whispering against her skin. Too cruel.

When his journey reached the beltline of her jeans, he tugged her T-shirt just high enough to allow his tongue to lap her stomach, her muscles clenching so tight as though that could somehow rein in the waves of pleasure rocketing through her body, keeping herself safe. Intact.

When his tongue dived to lick into her belly button she knew there was no holding back. Nowhere to hide. Nowhere safe. She was going over the edge and there would be no safety net.

Inch by inch her T-shirt scooted higher up her torso. She hung onto the back of the sofa so hard her knuckles hurt. Inch by inch he traversed her naked stomach with his mouth, his lips, his tongue, his teeth until she was panting with pleasure.

And then her T-shirt was gone. And her bra with it. Screwed up into a ball and tossed somewhere behind her. All two hundred dollars' worth of cotton and lace treated as if they meant nothing. But in that moment he could have thrown her boots into the fire and she couldn't have cared less.

It was a few moments before she realised Saxon was no longer tearing at her clothes. His hips pressed into hers, but he was tilted just enough so that he could look at her. Exposed, naked to the waist, her hair a mess, her breath heavy, her limbs lax, her skin hot and pink, clinging to him in the bright daylight. His eyes slid back to hers and she had never in her whole life felt more vulnerable.

'You are the sweetest woman I have ever met,' he said, his voice deep and croaky, shaking his head as though none of this was expected. As though it hadn't been building for days. And as though she herself was beyond belief.

She tilted her chin. 'I'm far from sweet.'

'Are you telling me you know my business better than I do?' he asked, his gaze sweeping back over her naked torso. His right hand lifted and hovered heartlessly mere millimetres from her left breast and all efforts at appearing cool dissolved.

She wished she could drudge up a funny retort, a hint of levity to take the edge of the dark, dangerous, spicy aura of passion weaving its spell around her, but the glint in his gorgeous eyes made it impossible.

He looked back into her eyes as he slid a wide flat

palm across her stomach turning her insides to liquid. He reached her beltline of her jeans. The button popping through the loop felt like a tiny little death all on its own. The sound of her zipper split the silence. His eyes didn't leave hers as his finger twisted and slipped below, making her breaths shudder from her lungs as he caressed, cajoled, teased, learnt her curves and most tender angles.

The pleasure was so vast and all-encompassing she wanted to cry out. But she couldn't spare the energy, for her whole world was focussed on his eyes. The heat, the desire and the raw, honest tenderness. And on every unexpected shift of his ingenious hand.

And then he was on his knees before her and…

He tugged down her jeans, and her G-string with them, and she was only just lucid enough to know to step out of them. His hands slid back up her legs. He kissed her knees, her thighs. He shifted his knee between her feet, setting them apart. A sheen of sweat broke out on her skin. She could taste it on her upper lip.

His thumb skimmed across her core. Gently once. Twice. Then again with more pressure. And again and again. And then just when she thought it couldn't get any better, his mouth replaced his thumb. He kissed her softly, as though marking his place. As though introducing himself. As though giving her a taste of things to come.

And soon she couldn't see anything at all past the shimmer surrounding her. It was as though her aura had gone into overdrive. The world was hazy, pink, pulsing. A mix of colours as she had never seen before. Colours so rich, and fleeting, and beautiful they tore at her heart.

Her toes curled into the floor. Her knuckles ached.
Her arms and legs were on fire. Waves of escalating
pleasure shimmied through her body from one end of
her to the other, crashing in on themselves until everything met in the very centre of her being.

Then the world turned red. Dark, hot, deep blood-
red. She let go of the couch and buried her hands in his
hair and soared higher, stronger, harder than she ever
had before until she hit the crest, rode the wave for so
long she thought she might pass out.

And then everything melted away into a pool of
liquid heat. Her fingers knotted into his too-long hair,
letting the tension and release spread from her fingertips and to him.

But it wasn't over yet. Saxon kissed his way up her
stomach, leaving hot, wet trails over her already damp
skin. She fumbled with his button fly, her shaking
fingers making hard work of it until he reached down
and tore them off in far less time than she would have
managed.

He slid on a condom, which he must have had
secreted somewhere on his person. When he'd brought
her here, and he had known exactly what he planned to
do to her.

He hefted her onto the back of the couch, and in one
solid thrust was inside her. So deep she cried out. But
it was all pleasure. Hot, hard, fabulous pleasure.

She hooked her legs tight around his hips, looped her
hands around his neck, and arched back as far as she
possibly could, trusting him implicitly to hold her and
giving him all the leverage he needed to drive deep
inside her.

She held on tight, not wanting any of this to ever end.

But he'd reached breaking-point. He drove so deep she could feel the power of it in her abdomen. Ecstasy and exquisite intimacy spun tight around them as Morgan felt him spilling into her.

And then all of a sudden her gasps took on a fever pitch, which evolved into an almighty cry as for the first time in her life Morgan came twice in ten minutes. For the first time in her life she'd found a man with talent enough to make it happen. Or perhaps for the first time in her life she'd found a man with whom she could let go, completely, and allow herself to let it happen.

Saxon gathered her into his arms. His mouth met hers and endless tenderness swamped her. And for the first time in her life Morgan Kipling-Rossetti was very much on the way to falling in love.

Heaven help her.

An hour later Morgan lay on her stomach. Naked. The sheets and quilt were pooled and twisted somewhere at the end of Saxon's wondrous, large, soft bed. But she didn't move to tidy them up. To hide the evidence of her indulgence. Her chin rested on her hands as she lay in the decadent thrall of disorder.

Outside the curtain-free window the world was white and the temperature below freezing. An icy wind shook snow from the spindly branches. But inside she was as warm as toast. Her blood had begun to flow from her centre and back to her extremities. Her focus remained fuzzy as she stared into the crackling fire in the wall of Saxon's cosy bedroom. She felt so relaxed, so comfortable and peaceful she could have lain there until the end of time.

'I've never had a woman climax in French before.'

Morgan shifted her head sideways, resting her cheek on the back of her left hand. Saxon came back from the kitchen with a couple of glasses of what looked and smelled like espresso coffee. He had pulled his jeans back on, but the top two buttons of his fly remained undone. A trail of dark hair arrowed from his belly button down the sexiest stomach she had ever laid eyes on.

If he came any closer she planned to reach out, hook a finger into his jeans and tug. But if he didn't come any closer she knew she didn't have near enough energy to do so. 'The real question is, have they done so in English?'

'Once or twice,' he admitted, a grin creasing his face as he put the hot drinks carefully onto the bedside table. 'But French? That is something I could really get used to.'

Morgan didn't press him. She wasn't sure how much French he might know. High school ABCs or far too much for comfort? Especially since, in the state she had been in when they'd moved to the bedroom and extraordinarily continued what they had started, she wasn't entirely sure what she had admitted aloud, in any language.

The mattress sank at her side as he sat next to her and ran a flat palm over her feet, up her calves, dipping between her thighs. Her breath hitched in her throat as he reached ever higher, but then he moved back to the rounded mounds of her buttocks, then slowly, gently, up the flat muscles of her back.

She caught him watching her watching him and it made her blush. 'I don't do this, you know,' she said, burying her face into the bed.

'Do what exactly? This?' he asked, before leaning over and kissing down each bump in her spine.

Her head lifted off the bed as though he'd hit a nerve that gave him complete control over her body. Her eyes dropped closed as suddenly her skin felt far too heavy for her to hold up. 'Nah,' she whispered, 'I do that all the time.'

His hands crept up the bed either side of her as he reached her neck. As he nibbled on the tendons of her shoulders his hands rested either side of her breasts, his thumbs stroking.

'But the rest,' she said on a sigh, 'let's just say it's not my usual Thursday afternoon with a practical stranger.'

'Meaning I'm special?' he asked, his warm breath creating goose-bumps all over her skin.

'Meaning you're some kind of sorcerer.' She curled her toes to fend off the almost painful sensation.

'So you're saying you've come under my spell.' He pushed away so that he could lie beside her, his whole body rubbing against her back, chest hair, hot skin, sinew, muscle and abrasive denim scraping against her skin, before he managed to find himself a comfortable spot beside her, leaning his head on his upturned hand.

She turned to face him, a curtain of messy hair shielding her from the potency of his gaze. Naturally he had a spare hand with which to push it back off her face, splaying it across her back, tucking one last strand behind her ear, every move making her need for breath stronger. 'I'm saying—'

'I know what you're saying, Morgan.' His eyes narrowed as she watched him, but he still smiled, confident in himself to the last. 'And thank you. That only makes it even more exceptional. If that is at all possible.'

She swallowed to clear the sudden lump in her throat. It was either that or sigh, and she had no intention of letting him know *how* exceptional on her part. For, despite her need for him to know she wasn't a wanton sex goddess all the time, this was what it looked like. A Thursday-afternoon special.

She lived in Paris; he lived in Melbourne. She needed a port in the storm and he needed to keep her on side. It was a relationship of mutual gain. And mutual risk. It could and would never be any more. She repeated the last sentence in her head three times to make sure she believed it.

'What's this?' she asked, fingering the silver medallion he always wore around his neck. It felt warm, nestled as it had been against his skin. It also gave her something else to focus on bar his beautiful, perceptive brown eyes.

Saxon pressed his chin against his chest, his mouth turning into that sexy gangster-movie frown he did so well, as he tried to see the symbol on the end of the short chain.

'Here,' he said, laying out his arm, indicating for her to lie in the nook. After a moment, a moment in which she could have refused, she could have pretended not to have understood, she could have saved herself from further intimacy, she gave in and snuggled against his chest and looked up at the medallion he was holding up to the flickering firelight.

'This,' he said, his deep voice resonating through her chest, 'is St Christopher. The patron saint of travellers.'

'So why do you wear it?'

'My mother gave it to me when I bought my first car.'

'You bought it? Yourself?'

He nodded. 'I worked three whole summers through high school to earn enough money to buy a truly dilapidated Datsun 120Y my cousin Mario wanted to sell me. In the end it turned out I'd earned enough for a nice little second-hand Monaro. I didn't find out until about ten years and three cars later that my father had in fact paid half and never let on. He'd wanted me to know the value of earning my own money, but he'd also wanted his son to come home safe and sound every night.'

He let go of the medal and lay back, his arms behind his head. Morgan shuffled to rest her head in the dip of his shoulder and continued to play with the medal, her fingers making continued contact with the skin of his chest at the same time.

'What was your first car?' he asked, his voice rumbling against her ear.

Morgan wasn't all that sure she wanted to say. She'd been given her sports Mercedes as a matter of a status symbol to appease her mother's friends. She hadn't found out until after *he* died that her father had worked overtime to pay for it. And it was one of the tainted luxuries she'd turned her back on when she'd moved to Paris and started her life afresh.

But now she was back. Here. And nothing was really afresh. It had all just been put on the back burner, heating and melting and getting closer and closer to boiling point. She shuffled to get deeper into the groove of Saxon's body. 'I don't remember,' she lied. 'It was something blue.'

He laughed. 'Women and cars. It has to be something genetic that means you don't care and we do.'

'To the point of naming yours, you mean. That's just strange.'

'Not so strange. Women like to name pets and teddy bears, men like to name other things.'

A grin spread across his face and she knew exactly what he was trying to say. She wondered what he called his. Something potent, and Italian for sure. Like Rocky, or Vulcan the Roman god of fire.

'Yep,' he said, 'we men like to name cars, and…race-horses. Things like that. Half the beauty of men and women are those very differences.'

'Vive la différence?'

'Exactly. The French don't do much better than the Italians, but they certainly got that part right.'

Saxon trailed his free arm down her side, over her hip, to the dent at the side of her left buttock and back up to her shoulder. He nonchalantly watched the path of his fingers, while Morgan's breath rose and fell in huge swells.

'Tell me about your wife,' she said, before she'd even felt the words forming. Saxon's caress came to a majestic halt. Morgan bit her lip and closed her eyes shut tight and hoped he would just pretend he hadn't heard her.

When his stroking began again, she thought she might have got away with it. Until he asked, 'What would you like to know?'

'I don't actually know why I even brought it up,' she admitted. 'A few people mentioned her today, that's all. In passing. And somehow now seemed as good a time as any to talk about her.'

While I am lying naked in your arms… Oh, God. Morgan made to shift away, but Saxon had seen it coming. His hand tucked beneath her hair, curling it around his fingers and then letting it spill across her back, and his chest. It felt so fabulous she simply couldn't move.

'Her name was Adriana,' he finally said. 'She was a beautiful Italian girl my parents had sponsored to come over from Italy to help with marketing of the business. We married, then we divorced four years ago last May. She went back home, and I stayed and spent every waking hour fixing the problems we had caused together.'

She heard the big fat full stop, as though that was the end of that. But he'd only opened up a whole new slew of questions she just had to know the answer to. Adele Cosgrove had seen some similarity in her, enough to make the comparison. She had to know what went wrong.

'What kinds of problems?'

'She wanted to upgrade, to bring the business into the twenty-first century. In doing so we lost our identity in a blur of stainless-steel fixtures and hot-pink décor that made us look like every new chain store on the east coast. The wonderful thing that had made us special was lost. Business stalled. We threw in good money after bad to no avail. And it was a very dark period for my family.'

'But you've come out the other side again, right? Sixty shopfronts. A private plane?'

He didn't say anything. He seemed lost in thought.

'And the *new* décor is just…gorgeous,' she said brightly, hoping to bring him back out again. To get some sort of idea if he truly was out the other side mentally and emotionally. If not… 'Who designed it?'

'It is reminiscent of the original shop, but my mother looked after all of the decoration, even going so far as to import fixtures from her home town in Italy.'

'It worked,' Morgan said. 'The place really does have a magic about it. A warm and comfortable beauty. Do tell her I think she has a wonderful eye.'

'You should tell her yourself.' Saxon was being sassy. But it only made Morgan's chest squeeze so tight it hurt to breathe.

They both knew she could never tell his mother anything. She was his dirty secret. Who she was, what they were up to here, and what she was up to back in Melbourne. Morgan's feet suddenly felt cold. She tucked them under a corner of the comforter and moved on.

'Are the other fifty-nine the same?'

'Pretty much.'

'So what if I went ahead with my plans to create a new precinct, and I guaranteed *you* a prime ground-level position?' She lifted up onto her elbows and flapped her hands in the air as her excitement grew. 'The design the architects have come up with is so beautiful. You should see it. And you know business far better than I do, so you could be like an advisor on the project. Help me to do it right.'

But what she was asking him was so much more. What she was really asking was what he thought about being her man in Melbourne while the project went through. For she would have to come back, monthly even, to oversee the construction. Perhaps even to take on a hands-on role in the choice of fixtures and fittings. Lending her expert eye to create a piece of bohemian Montmartre in the heart of little Italy. It could work. It could be amazing.

Saxon breathed in deep through his nose while Morgan waited for him to make his decision. It felt as if it were the most important decision of her life, and the fact that it wasn't hers to make terrified her.

'And the others?' he finally asked.

'The who? What?' she said, trying to disentangle herself from the fantasy of being able to catch up with Saxon monthly. To be able to see him, touch him, kiss him, make love to him…

'The Changs,' he said. 'The Cosgroves. The Purans. And Jan.'

'Truthfully, I don't think they'll be able to afford it.' She shifted and her hair became caught under her elbow, so that she had to tug it free in a wholly ungraceful manoeuvre. 'And I don't know how any of their particular businesses would fit into the boutique atmosphere we have in mind. And what would they do for three months in the interim?'

Saxon shifted his head so she had to look into his eyes. But he said nothing. He simply let her words spin back and slap her across the back of the head. This was what he had been trying to tell her all this time. That she would be sending good, kind, hard-working people out on their ear. Well, that couldn't be the be-all and end-all. Didn't *her* interests matter too? Maybe the great glaring truth she kept refusing to see was that they didn't matter to him.

Now it wasn't only her feet that felt cold. Every inch of exposed skin felt kissed by a sudden chill.

'It's not my place to hold their hand through this, Saxon. The world turns and you have to turn with it or you'll fall off the edge. One way or the other, things will not stay as they are. I was lumped with this place, and you'll all be lumped with my decision. *C'est la vie.*'

His dark eyes bore into hers. She set her jaw and

stared back. Her legs were still entangled in his. Her hair
trailed across his chest. His hand rested on her hip, but
they were no longer really together.

'Whatever happened to the old-fashioned niceties?'
he asked. 'Whatever happened to loving thy neighbours?'

'You have no idea what an anomaly you are, Saxon.'
Her voice shook. She hated that her voice shook. She
hated that this guy made her feel so much that her
nerves got the better of her. But that didn't stop her. She
had things to say. 'You have a family who love you. A
huge family. I have a mother I haven't seen in nearly
ten years. A woman who didn't have the dignity to
mourn my father's death as he deserved to be mourned.
A woman who married her husband's best friend within
months of her husband's death. That's it. That's *all* the
family I have.'

Saxon's dark eyes glimmered with such sudden
sorrow she felt it slice through her, hot and devastatingly
comforting. He moved up onto his left elbow and tried
to reach up to cup her face but she pushed his hand
away.

'You have neighbours you have known for years,' she
continued, 'who would put a new bulb in if they noticed
your front light went out, who would bring you dinner
if they saw you were working after hours. I've spent my
adult life living in apartments in rundown buildings in
a part of town you wouldn't want to walk through alone
at night, and if my heat got cut off, I had nobody who
gave a damn.'

'Morgan,' Saxon said, his voice ragged. He tried to
comfort her again. Tried to touch her. But she pulled
away. She sat up and dragged at the sheet to cover her

breasts, leaving him bare to the waist. Bare, buff and beautiful. Like an angel. Like a god. Her breath hitched in her throat, her heart stampeded through her chest, and her stomach threatened to roll over on itself. But she pushed the reactions to the back of her mind. She was vulnerable enough. And she wasn't even close to finished.

'But now,' she said, her voice thready, 'now I have a steady job, I have clothes on my back, I have people who know me, two of whom won't stop calling me in case I was thinking of disappearing. And though it's far from perfect I *don't* want to lose all of that. I can't. I can't go back to having nothing and nobody and with the costs I would incur keeping Como Avenue as is I would go under and fast. And my only choice would be to slink back here. To her. And that would just kill me.'

She felt the streak of tears sliding hot and fast down her cheeks. She didn't want to cry. But the emotion of the past week finally got to her. Her grandfather's death, having to travel back to Melbourne, her mother's messages, Alicia's over-the-top anxiety, coming against a force field the likes of the Como Avenue gang, and now this. A night of making love to a strong, solid, honest, generous man who complicated things so badly he made everything else seem simple.

Saxon sat up. He reached out and his hand dived beneath her hair. This time she didn't have the strength to push him away. Instead she turned into his arms. She cried, and fell apart, and let him kiss her. Her mouth wet with salty tears. It felt so…much, so strong, so deep. If not for his steady hand at the back of her neck, she would have simply collapsed into a pile of jelly.

But he held her upright, he held her to him, and he

kissed her again and again. Sweet, tender, bountiful kisses. Followed by slow, purposeful, meaningful kisses full of apology, and regret, and blooming sexual appetite.

He turned her then, laying her back against the bed. She let the sheet slip away and used her hands for better purposes, reaching around his neck to pull him to her. Her fingers diving beneath layers of soft dark hair.

His heaviness weighed upon her, pressing the air from her lungs, until he shifted, sliding his leg along hers, carrying his weight upon his knee, his elbow. She opened her eyes to see him pulling back to gently push the damp strands of her hair off her hot forehead. Wiping away the tracks of her forgotten tears.

He looked down into her eyes. His were like dark chocolate. Like deep wells filled with more knowledge and experience than she would ever hope to know. She only wished they were filled with something else. Promise? Hope? Love?

'I'm making your life a living hell right now, aren't I?' he asked.

'Well, not right now,' she said, brushing his hair off his forehead, drinking in the sight of him poised above her. Big. Beautiful. A man who had spoiled her for all others. God, if he only knew the hell she was in. Knowing now with blinding clarity that she was in love with him. A man who would have no choice but to break her heart.

'Mmm,' he grumbled. 'That's something, at least.'

He kissed her. For what felt like hours.

And again they made love. This time it was slow, and intimate, and careful, as though both of them were trying to wipe away the unspoken knowledge that there really was no way out of the fix they had found themselves in.

'Everything will be okay,' he promised much later as she began to fall asleep in his arms.

And with a long, ragged sigh Morgan closed her eyes, nestled into his arms and did her very best to believe him.

CHAPTER EIGHT

AS USUAL Saxon woke at dawn.

Sleeping Beauty looked so peaceful he left her to her forty winks and after a quick shower upstairs so as not to wake her he headed to the ski shed out the back of the cabin.

Once inside he decked himself out in a top-to-toe red and black ski suit and hot-green goggles, which no doubt would freak Morgan out if she realised that he really was 'one of them'. He grinned as he grabbed his snow board and shuffled off to the nearby ski-lift.

At the peak of the mountain he stretched his shoulders, breathed in deep and looked out over the acres of blinding white. Everything always seemed so clear to him when he came up here. Virgin snow. No foot-prints. Standing on top of the world. It always made his concerns seem insignificant.

He waited for that same clarity to come to him now. With the gentle ambient sound of high-altitude winds in his ears. The serene swaying of trees pocking the terrain. The soft slip and lift of fresh snow caught in the soft morning breeze.

But all he could think about was Morgan lying warm

and willing in his bed. All long, slim limbs, soft parted lips, and skin like velvet.

He'd had no particular intention of coming up here the day before. His bag was *always* packed in the back of his car so he could take off up the snow the moment he had a free day. But when she'd jumped in his car and said she was willing to go wherever he took her, he'd simply followed the road as long as she'd let him.

The road had, oh, so kindly led him to a night in her arms. And even more surprisingly, inside her head. Her confused, anguished, sympathetic, passionate, scared, beautiful head.

Morgan was not a situation he could solve by simple clarity. The waters between them were muddied by far too many factors now. By his needs. And hers. And those of a hundred other people. And by the fact that he was crazy about her.

Yet to get what he needed he would have to hurt her. And to give her what *she* needed he would be sacrificing his family's trust he'd worked so hard to rebuild. There was no way he could win the girl and win the war. He knew that going into this. So why did it suddenly feel so unfair?

The only thing that did become clear was that the top of a mountain was the last place he wanted to be.

He strapped himself into his snow board, snapped his wrist guards into place, bent his knees, angled his legs just so and took off down the steep slope, the need to concentrate on not getting killed dulling all other thoughts. Bar one.

When he hit the bottom he was going straight home to her.

* * *

Once Saxon had left his gear in the shed out the back, he peered through the bedroom window to find it was empty. Only tangled white sheets and a dent in the spare pillow told him Morgan had ever really been there.

He continued around to the back door, shook the snow off his jeans and T-shirt and padded inside in bare feet.

And there he found Morgan sitting on the window seat looking out through the spindly snow gums to the ski fields beyond. Her feet were hooked onto the bench, her arms hugging her knees. She wore one of his navy jumpers, the ends of the arms hanging beyond her fingertips, the length covering her legs so that only her small feet with their racy red toenails poked out the end. Her gorgeous hair was its usual tumble of waves down her back.

Saxon's chest gave a sharp thump at the sight. It turned his mouth dry. It had been some time since he had come home to a woman in his room. In his clothes. In his life. And never once had it been a woman like this one.

Images of the night before overlapped one another in his mind. Her soft, supple skin beneath his fingers, the taste of her on his tongue, and the energy and release with which she came. And the subtle sadness in her eyes when she'd not realised he was watching her. He wished he'd known her longer to know how much of that sadness had been put there by him.

He ran a hand over his face, rasping against stubble, and pulled himself together. 'Good morning,' he called out as he rubbed his hands together and joined her in the lounge room.

She gave a little start, before smiling gently up at him. 'You've been skiing?'

'Snow boarding. Fabulous way to kick-start the day.'

He leaned down and kissed the top of her head. 'Hungry?'

'Famished,' she said. She slid her feet out from under her until they hit the floor, leaving her legs now bare to the thigh.

Saxon's skin warmed a good degree. After the night they'd had he would have been surprised if he'd even considered sex again for a good long while. But he'd thought wrong. Where this woman was concerned it seemed his appetite was not even close to being satiated.

'Stay,' he said, running a hand down her waves, a lock sliding through his fingers before he let it drop and settle among the rest. 'I'll cook. You just relax.'

He headed over to the kitchen and wasn't all that surprised when he heard her soft footfalls behind him. She was not the kind of girl to ever do as he asked. And this time it only made him smile.

He reached into the fridge and pulled out some eggs, long-life milk, and a resealable bag of pre-grated cheese, the single man's staple supplies.

She slid onto a barstool on the opposite side of the bench and watched him. He was surprised to find her brow was furrowed. He shook it off and put it down to morning-after jitters. He could fix that.

'So,' he said as he tossed four eggs into a frying-pan. 'I was thinking that after breakfast we could snuggle together on the banana lounges outside and laugh at the novice skiers while drinking schnapps and eating melted marshmallows.'

'I thought…' She cleared her throat and looked down at her fingernails. 'I assumed we'd head straight back to Melbourne.'

Saxon stopped mid egg-shuffle.

'This trip was unexpected,' she said, her cheeks warming, her eyes glancing at him and then away again nervously.

'You have other…arrangements again?'

She shrugged. 'I do need to call home about something.'

'Home?'

'Paris.'

Right, he thought, *home*. 'Eat first, then we go?'

She nodded. Blinked. 'Sure. Fine. Whatever.'

He stopped whisking and watched her. She wasn't spitting venom, but neither was she sweeter than a sugar cone. She was acting…neutral.

He opened his mouth to talk to her about last night. To reassure her… That it was a mistake? That it wasn't? That it was a one-off deal? Or that he wanted her in his arms and in his bed again that night? And the next and the next. That he was prepared to take her deal if it meant she'd look him in the eye again? Or that their time together didn't change anything?

Not having one clue which of those was the whole truth, he shut his mouth and took to whisking again with a vengeance.

The drive back to Melbourne was tougher than the drive to the snow, even though Morgan wasn't ranting at him the whole way. Her silence was far more worrying. It brought back his itch tenfold. He scratched the back of his hands, one at a time.

Maybe he was allergic to her. He damn well hoped not, especially after what they had been up to the night before. He shifted on his seat all the same.

A half-hour later she was still at it. Mutely staring

out the window. He couldn't stand it. Though it was his nature to shoulder his burdens himself, it wasn't in his blood to be this quiet for this long. 'Morgan, look at me.'

She turned her head to face him. Her great green eyes looked so doleful he nearly ran the car off the road.

He looked back to the front and gripped the steering wheel tighter. *First things first.* 'Can we talk about Como Avenue? Seriously? No games. No hysterics.'

When she said nothing he glanced at her to find her staring at him in bemusement. He held a hand to his chest. 'From me. I meant no hysterics from me.'

Her cheeks lifted as she laughed softly, and his heart did a happy somersault in his chest. 'So what are our options, as you see them?' he asked.

She breathed in deep through her nose and looked past him to the trees whipping by the window. 'Barton had plans approved to knock the place down and build a two-storey complex. Investors were in place before he died. They have the first right of refusal on any development or future sale. And they are still willing to back me if I am willing to sell the land to them for quite a nice price in nine years. Or, I need to raise the rent by twenty-five per cent.'

Saxon opened his mouth to protest but she cut him off with a waggle of her finger.

'Twenty-five per cent,' she said. 'Minimum. Barton was a rich old bastard. Maybe he saw helping you lot out as some kind of back door into heaven.'

Saxon changed down a gear and risked taking his eyes off the road again. 'You don't need a back door into heaven?'

'No,' she said, her slight smile growing just enough

that he felt it hit him in the chest like Cupid's arrow. 'I don't. I've gone out of my way to keep out of other people's way so that nobody got hurt. I'll be just fine.'

He turned back to the road, changed up a gear again and picked up his speed so as to overtake a campervan. 'So for you to come out of this mess ahead, you need to knock us down brick by brick or bleed us dry dollar by dollar.'

'Yeah, that's my evil plan. Now if you'd only listened when I told you all this the first time think how much time we would have saved,' Morgan said.

Saxon turned onto busy Brunswick Street and kept his eyes dead ahead as he hit trams and traffic. He waited until he slowed for a red light before turning to Morgan and saying, 'And how much fun we would have missed.'

She tucked her bottom lip into her mouth and blushed like a virgin milkmaid. And Saxon was absolutely certain he couldn't have found her one mite sexier if she'd actually been dressed like one.

Then after a pause she did as Saxon had very much hoped. She asked, 'So what would it take for you to be convinced that your little collective will come out of this okay?'

He took a moment. He needed to say this right. No games. No hysterics. And no bull. 'They can't afford a raise in rent, not one that immense. Even if they agreed to let me cover it, that would not be a long-term solution. Not if it meant eating into my family's holdings as well as my own. And if you move them on, they won't have the capital to start afresh, refit, build clientele, et cetera. They will suffer.'

'What about a loan? Like a business loan. Or what

if my partners can back you up on that? What if I make it a term of the investment that they have to provide relocation funding to the five shopfronts?' Her voice came out louder and quicker as she ran with the idea.

'They won't go for it, Morgan.'

'You can't know that.'

'Faceless investors aren't nice, that's why they're faceless. They don't need to make bold gestures in order to keep everybody happy. Besides, it's not just about the money.'

She threw her arms in the air. 'Oh, come on, Saxon. You're just making this far harder than it needs to be. It is about the money. It's always about money. People make crap decisions based on nothing but money all the time.'

'This is about history, Morgan.'

'History my right butt cheek. You're just stubborn and pigheaded and when Adriana burnt you, she burnt you good and proper. Move on already.' Morgan glared at him, her eyes blazing.

It sent off a boatload of fireworks in his chest, the resultant kick of energy infusing him with sudden roaring passion. Passion enough to stop the car and jump her then and there. Or passion enough to stop the car and tell her to get out and walk?

'Like you've moved on?' he shot back, deliberately keeping the car on the move. 'Like you've been able to put aside your differences with your mother and visit since you've been here?'

'Excuse me?'

'History is *everything*. You won't visit your mother as she hurt you too badly. And you're right, I won't let you take those good people down after they stood by me.'

She shook her fists at the ceiling. 'I don't know why I even bothered to try to make you see things my way.'

'We *can't* just agree to disagree.'

'That's right,' she said. 'I hold all the cards. It's my decision. And I'm going to be the one to make it. And that's that.'

They hit Lygon Street wrapped in loaded silence. He knew she was deliberately not looking at the Como Avenue shopfronts as she directed him to where she had parked her rental car, only to find it was no longer there.

She got out of Bessie before he'd even turned off the engine. 'It was here. I know it was here. I remember the white picket fence and the red roses. Dammit!' she shouted, clenching her fists at her sides. She was so worked up he could almost see her aura turning blue.

He poked his head out the car window and saw the yellow markings on the footpath. He couldn't help but laugh at the irony. 'It's a no-parking zone unless you have a Local Residence Permit, Morgan. The car's been towed.'

'Of course it has. It's just one great big cosmic joke after another.'

'There have been more?'

She looked at him then. Really looked at him. Her eyes wild and stunning. Her shoulders rising and falling with her fury. And she said, 'You have no idea.'

'Just let me take you home, Morgan,' he said.

'Not unless this thing has wings and a tank of gas large enough to cross an ocean.' She began to shiver as the Antarctic wind seeped through her clothing, but she still stood there as though hoping her rental car would materialise out of thin air.

'Just get back in. I'll take you back to your hotel

where you can stew and stomp and hate me all you like in the comfort of a centrally heated room. Okay?'

She thought about it. The stubborn piece of work actually stood there in near-zero temperature and thought about it. Then she hoisted the door open and huddled in the far edge of the seat as he drove her back to her inner-city hotel.

She got out and slammed the door the second they arrived, and he sat, idling, watching her jog into the hotel. Amazed that she didn't trip herself up in her bright blue high-heeled boots. Watching her long wavy hair swing left to right with each step. Realising she still wore his navy jumper.

He wondered if he might ever see her again to get it back. He wondered if he might ever see her again period. And the thought that he might have blown it, that he might have been prioritising things in his life in such a way as to push a woman like her away for ever, sat like a lump of cold coal in his chest.

It took three swipes with the key card for Morgan to unlock her hotel room door. Once she finally got inside she dumped the plastic bag filled with her poncho and yesterday's underwear to the floor, and dragged her feet to the bed where she slumped there upon. Face down. Mouth full of quilted bedspread.

She needed to go back to Paris where there was no chance of snow for another six months. Where people respected her, meaning they did as she told them to do. Where the only regular man in her life wore leather pants, fake glasses, and carried a man bag.

But she couldn't do that until she'd made a decision on the Como Avenue shops. Up the rent and lose most of the retailers and end up making less money on the place than she was now? Or knock the place down, and lose them all. Jan and her cave of wonders. The crazy fighting Cosgroves. The kindly Changs. The keen-to-please Purans. She barely knew any of them, but when she hadn't been paying attention they'd found their way under her skin. And the thought of taking them down in order to pick herself up made her feel ill.

Though she hated to admit it she needed help making this decision. From someone she could trust.

Saxon. His name rose unbidden into her thoughts. But she *couldn't* trust him, no matter how hard her sorry heart was convincing her to try. They were on opposite sides of this war.

Morgan spun onto her back, stared at the ceiling and spat a lump of hair from her mouth.

She was in love with him. When had she let that happen? When he'd held her in his arms as she'd cried over her lame duck of a family? When she'd seen inside his beautiful cabin in the snow and felt as if she could comfortably lay her hat there for ever? When he'd first stood up to her by bringing all and sundry to their non-date? Or when she'd first looked up and seen him behind the Bacio Bacio counter, rough, ready, and gorgeous enough to warm even the most brittle heart? Or each and every time he made her smile? Made her laugh?

She tilted her head sideways and saw that the red light on her hotel phone was flashing. With a groan she dragged herself into a sitting position.

She felt a sudden overwhelming desire to just run away. To a new place altogether. A fresh start. With no one connected to her in any way, shape or form. She'd done it before; she could do it again.

She ran her hands hard over her dry eyes and let out a long, sorry for herself sigh. When she was seventeen and heart-broken, running and hiding had been a matter of survival. But now, older, and hopefully wiser, it just seemed the easy way out.

She sat up, and pushed her hair off her face, then caught her image in the reflection of a gilded mirror on the wall. Gone were the dark rings under her tired eyes that she usually hid behind mascara and huge sunglasses. Gone was the perpetual frown. Gone were the stiff neck, and uptight shoulders, and aching feet that she lived with every long, hard day spent running around after pouting models and temperamental photographers.

And gone were her usual armour of I'm-too-cool-for-you designer clothes as she sat there engulfed in Saxon's navy jumper. She reached up and folded a handful inside a soft fist. It felt expensive, like the softest new wool. She wondered how often he'd worn it. How often it had rested neat and tight around his solid chest. How often it had slipped along his warm skin.

She let her eyes drift closed, then slid her arms around her torso until she was hugging herself. For a few lovely moments she allowed herself to think it was his arms, his hug. She even imagined she could still smell his scent wrapped around her. Deliciously hot and sweet.

But they weren't his arms. They weren't his hands. It wasn't his embrace. She was alone, and he was somewhere else. And this was how it would feel when she went back to Paris.

Her eyes drifted open, and she saw that they were welling with tears. She sniffed deep, uncurled her arms from around her and ran a finger swiftly beneath each eye.

She had to get over this, over him, and fast. And there was only one way she could think to do so. To remind herself why her heart had been used for not all that much more than pumping blood for a good decade. She picked up the phone, and called the one person she couldn't believe she now saw as the lesser of two evils.

The phone answered. A feminine clearing of the throat was followed by a simple, 'Hello.'

Morgan felt tears again prick the backs of her eyes, though these tears were hot, and bitter and a decade in the making.

'Mum,' she croaked. 'Mum, it's me. Morgan.'

The bell over the Bacio Bacio door rang. Saxon looked up from the pile of mail he was flicking through, his heart thrumming against his ribs in anticipation. It was a pretty blonde. But not the blonde he had been hoping for.

'Good afternoon,' he said.

'So it is,' she returned, smiling at him from beneath pretty eyelashes as she swung equally pretty hips towards the glass casings.

But there was no zing. No crackle. No spice. All the zing and crackle and spice he had room for in his life was holed up alone in some city hotel.

Vincent came in from the back room carrying a box of new red napkins Saxon's mum had designed. He pulled one out and laid it on the counter. The two x's Saxon had insisted everyone carve into the lattes were printed in gold in a corner of the napkin.

'Looks great, Dad,' Saxon said. It was perfect. The branding was spot on. But he couldn't quite bring himself to enthuse about it as much as he usually would.

'So how does this Sunday sound?' Vincent asked.

'Hmm?'

'For dinner. With your new girl. Your mother wanted me to tell you she has even planned a menu for her. High in carbohydrates.' Vincent patted his svelte stomach and grinned. He wasn't allowed to eat anywhere near as much food as his Italian blood desired since his heart attack. Special occasions were an exception.

'Sorry, Dad. I don't know that she'll be able to make it.'

'And why not?'

Why not? He didn't know where to begin.

'Sax, you have to stop doing this to yourself.'

'What's that?'

'None of us are blind, you know,' Vincent said. 'We all know how much work you have put into this place over the past few years. How much of yourself. And we all know why. Perhaps we let you do it for the first little while as you seemed to need to so very much. But now your reasons for hanging on so tight are no longer there. It's come to the point where we are only taking advantage. So let go. The time has come to invest as much energy into your personal life.' Vincent slapped him on the back. 'Your mother and I want grandkids, you know.'

The pretty blonde whom Saxon had forgotten was even there made a funny noise in the back of her throat before bolting from the store. But he didn't care. There was only one blonde he could even consider for the job, and that eventuality was as likely as his father breaking out into sudden cartwheels.

'Morgan's not coming to dinner, Dad.'

'Have you asked her?'

'Well. No.'

'And why not?'

'She's flighty. She's difficult. She's stubborn. She lives in Paris. And she drives me crazy.'

Vincent grinned. 'The best ones always do.'

Saxon blinked. 'You think?'

'I know we haven't talked about this all that much, but you and Adriana: did you ever fight?'

Saxon shook his head. 'Not so much. I think we drained one another with politeness. If we'd fought then maybe I could have avoided everything that went wrong in the end.'

'Maybe you could. Or maybe the two of you simply never had enough passion for it to be that way. Yet now, since this one has come on the scene… I haven't seen you this energised in years, my boy. It's brilliant. And it's all about the girl. Friction is passion. It's honesty. It's communication. And the make-up sex…' Vincent held out a hand and sent a small prayer of thanks to the heavens.

Saxon grinned. 'Yet, even so, I fear I may have played my cards all wrong.'

'Son, the way you play them is irrelevant. If your cards and hers are meant to end up in the same deck, it will just happen. Your mother and I were from different ends of Italy. We met in Rome. The both of us on holidays. The moment I saw her walking towards me across the Forum I knew. She knew. I could have plucked a flower from the roadside, I could have serenaded her; I could have teased her; I could have got down on my knee and proposed. It wouldn't have mattered. We were just meant to be.'

Meant to be? That seemed far too arbitrary for

Saxon's liking. But the way Morgan felt in his arms, the way she melted when they kissed, the way her eyes burned through him as if she knew exactly how much of his bravado was for real, and how much was for show, it certainly meant that she was very, *very* special.

If only they'd met one crazy summer afternoon walking towards one another in the Roman Forum... But unfortunately they weren't the cards they had been dealt.

'I'll let you know if things change, okay, Dad?' Saxon reached down and picked up the pile of bills.

Vincent pulled them out of his hands, wrapped them back in a rubber band and put a new red napkin around them and wrote in bold black pen: 'Darius, handle it.'

He gave Saxon's shoulder a squeeze. 'If not this Sunday, then another. We're in no hurry.'

Saxon watched his father leave, whistling a Bobby Darin tune. And he wondered, what would she say if he just asked? If he put some faith in himself, in his heart's ability to love the right person for him, and in her ability to fight against her history and trust him? What would she say if he asked her to stay? For Sunday lunch.

For ever.

Morgan sat on an overstuffed antique Edwardian chair, her back ramrod-straight as it was not the kind of chair one could lounge in. Not that she wanted to. She wanted to cross her arms, cross her legs, and bounce her foot up and down in displeasure.

While her mother's day maid poured the tea it gave her time to have a good look at the woman who had let her down so wholly all those years before.

She looked the same. Morgan even wondered if

she'd had work. But the longer she looked, the more fine lines and deep grooves gathered within Pamela's face. A face that her father had loved so much he had done everything she'd ever asked of him without question. Worked too hard. Pampered her too much. And died too young because of it.

'Don't tell me that's a Chanel,' Pamela said once they were alone.

Morgan glanced down at her black and white shag tartan jacket, which she was wearing over Calvin Klein jeans and a black and silver chain hipster belt from...who knew? Some fashion-shoot leftover on some cold night at three in the morning. Whoop-de-doo.

'It is,' she admitted. Though when she saw the pride in her mother's eyes she wished she could rip the clothes from her back and replace them with Kmart specials.

'It's lovely,' Pamela said. 'I mean, *you* are just so lovely. Far too thin, but that's what comes from living in Paris. I certainly was when I met your father there.'

Pamela picked up her china teacup with her pinkie finger poking out the side as if she had been taught at some deportment class her own mother had made her take. After an infuriatingly long sip she said, 'You never wrote back when I wrote you.'

'I was never the one to give you my address,' Morgan shot back.

Pamela shrugged and even managed to make that seem genteel. 'Your father's cousin owns a hardware store in St Germain. He found you in Montmartre within about two weeks of your arrival and kept tabs on you ever since.'

'You've kept in touch with Dad's family?' Morgan asked.

'Of course.'

'Do they know you remarried?'

'They do,' Pamela said, her eyes careful, watchful.

'They know who to?' Morgan asked, her voice so icy her lips felt cold. 'And how soon after?'

'Morgan, if you tell me you are still harbouring a grudge that I married Julian after all this time, then I'll be very disappointed.'

'Disappointed?' Morgan shot back, a luscious newfound fire lighting her from within. '*You'll* be disappointed in me? Well, sometimes people don't behave the way you expect them to. It's best you learn to live with it.'

Pamela flinched as though slapped. Her tea sloshed over the side leaving a growing brown stain on her crêpe skirt. 'Is this why you finally called me? In order to reopen old wounds? If it is then I'm going to have to ask you to leave.'

Morgan tipped forward on her chair, the urge to do just that pulling her only so far before she knew she couldn't. Saxon had accused her of letting history repeat itself. Well, she was going to prove him wrong.

'I…' This was so hard. She'd spent so many years being independent. Taking this leap, by choice, was like watching all that hard work unravel and doing nothing to stop it. 'No. I didn't come here to fight, or play the blame game. I called you because I need your advice.'

'My advice.'

Morgan uncurled her fingers from the seat and placed them on her knees, and took a deep breath. 'You know Grandad died, right?'

Something flickered behind Pamela's eyes. Sadness? Regret? The knowledge that Morgan was here doing what she'd never had the strength to do with her own father? Trying to make amends. Or at least bridge the gap. What a pathetic family bunch they made.

'I did know that,' Pamela said.

'Well, he left me a strip of five shopfronts on Como Avenue in Carlton.'

The flicker disappeared as a small smile lit Pamela's deep green eyes. It made her look ten years younger. Fun and defiant, the way she had been when Morgan had been growing up. The way that had made it so easy for her father to love her.

'What did he leave you?' Morgan asked.

'My mother's china,' Pamela said with a sigh as her gaze came to rest on the pretty Royal Doulton teaset on the table before them. 'The rest he left to a lost dogs' home in Mansfield. I haven't yet decided if I think it funny or just plain mean.'

'He gave me the proviso that I can't sell the land for nine years,' Morgan said. 'Yet he hadn't put up the rent at Como Avenue in ages. So if I put up the rent now in order to cover the costs, the tenants won't be able to afford it. But if I let the investors he had lined up knock the place down and build a bright, shiny, new precinct, the tenants will go out of business.'

Pamela laughed. 'Mean. Just as I thought. Do you think he died so he wouldn't have to make the decision himself?'

'Probably,' Morgan said. Then she was surprised to find a smile stretching her cheeks when she added, 'Though he cut you off when you married dad easily enough.'

Pamela held up her cup of tea in a salute. 'That he did. The old cur.'

Morgan wondered if her grandfather had left her the

property as he saw some of himself in her. For she, like him, had rejected her for making a decision she didn't agree with. Well, that was just depressing.

'I have no regrets in the way I have acted, Morgan,' Pamela said, as though she knew exactly where her thoughts had gone. 'Your father was the love of my life. And I knew I'd never love another the same. Julian is kind. And generous. And we have a good life. I no longer have to fight for the things I need to keep me comfortable where your father and I always struggled. He hated that I struggled; he always blamed himself for your grandfather cutting me off. But it was my choice; I knew what I was getting into. I loved him. That was enough.'

'So why the fancy house,' Morgan asked, leaning forward and resting her elbows on her knees, 'the fancy cars, the fancy trips to the snow?'

'Again, that was all your father. He loved looking after me. Looking after us. Denying him that pleasure only hurt him.'

Morgan pulled herself off the chair and paced the room, railing against her mother's words. They fitted far too neatly. And she'd spent far too long despising her. 'So why didn't you try harder to tell me all of this years ago?'

'You are my daughter, *chérie*.'

That stopped Morgan dead in her tracks: the endearment her father had always used. Her cheeks felt so hot she wished she could leave to splash water on her face, but if she left now she might never come back. And she had to do this. She needed to clear her heart. 'Meaning?'

'I was in the exact same boat myself thirty-odd years ago. My own father let me go, and with that gift I was able to become my own person, find my own path. I had no intention of denying you that no matter how many nights I cried myself to sleep when you left.'

Morgan glanced up at her mother to find tears welling in her eyes now. Eyes that looked so much like her own. Jade-green, tired, and so very, very sad. Or that was how her eyes had looked a week ago. Not so in the mirror that morning…

Morgan slumped back down into her chair.

'I am so proud of how far you have come in Paris, *chérie*,' Pamela said. 'I would never have been that brave.'

'You gave up an inheritance that could sink a ship to marry the man you loved. I'm afraid I don't have it in me to be *that* brave.'

Pamela clutched a fine lace hanky to her chest. 'Don't you dare tell me you are in love.'

'No,' Morgan shot back, too fast, too loud. Even she didn't believe herself. 'No,' she said again more gently.

'But there is a man. Tell me about him. Did you meet him in Paris? If you did you know I couldn't blame you.'

Morgan felt herself clamming up. She couldn't do this. She didn't like talking about herself, her feelings, for it meant she had some. But her mother looked so interested. Purely, honestly, interested. Her mother. Her only family.

The pull was far stronger than she'd imagined it could still be. Oh, who was she kidding? She'd come all the way to Australia on the request of a man she'd never met. Because he was blood. And looking into her mother's familiar eyes, she felt all her old disappointments drying up like old tears.

'No,' Morgan said, then had to clear her throat of the frog within. 'He lives here.'

Pamela blinked. 'Have you known him long?'

'Four days.'

'Four days,' Pamela repeated, her eyes lighting up. 'And the cycle begins again. I knew I loved your father in three. But you girls these days are far more independent and sensible than we ever were. Don't be too sensible. It's nowhere as much fun as playing against the odds.'

'Nothing I feel for him is sensible,' Morgan admitted, saying the words out loud making her feelings at once less scary, and more real.

Pamela laughed, a sweet sound that brought back so many warm memories, memories of her father twirling her mother in his arms when he came home from work, memories of lying in bed at night and listening to them talk and laugh as they headed past her room to theirs. Memories that made her feel connected, and soft, and comfortable, and all the more unravelled. 'That is wonderful news, Morgan.'

'No, it's not. It's unfortunate. And accidental. And unnerving. And bad timing. And impossible. And he's…he's just so stubborn, and talented, and he drives me around the bend.'

'And you are trying to convince me that you're not in love with him?'

Morgan opened her mouth to explain herself. But the words just wouldn't come out. She was about to pull the rug out from under him. How could she love a man and do that to him? But how could she love herself and not?

'He's a good man,' she said. 'A kind man. Generous to a fault. He should find himself a nice girl.'

'You're not a nice girl?'

'I'm a stubborn girl. Used to getting my own way. I don't know that the two can really mesh. More like collide.'

'He knows this about you—am I right?'

Morgan thought about it, then nodded. She'd hardly hidden the fact. In fact the two of them couldn't be in the same city without flinting sparks off one another.

'And he's still around?'

He'd more than stuck around. He'd pursued her from the moment he'd met her. She'd never known a man with such tenacity. And such hard-headedness. Who'd made such a focussed, unstoppable beeline for her.

'So you said you came here as you needed some advice,' Pamela said, letting her off the hook.

But she wasn't off the hook; she was so far on the hook it was now a part of her. Like a tattoo, a brand, a permanent fixture. She had fallen in love with Saxon Ciantar, a man she couldn't by any stretch of the imagination keep. Even if he felt the same way…

She'd worry about that later. Much later. Hopefully later enough that she might forget and it might go away on its own and she could go back to the life she'd enjoyed before she had come here, before she had met him. A life of late nights, hard work, rare friendships, no family ties, and nobody who filled her thoughts and her heart and made her browbeaten spirit take flight.

Morgan took a deep breath. 'I was wondering if Julian still worked in property law.'

At the mention of her husband's name Pamela looked stunned, but thankfully she held herself together. Morgan wasn't sure she could handle tears; this was all far too raw and demanding as it was.

Pamela nodded. 'He does.'

'Do you think he would mind if I talked to him about my ideas?' It still pained her to say it, it still pained her to even think there was another man in her father's place, but the thought of leaving here without taking her mother's olive branch felt far worse.

'I'll call him now, shall I?' Pamela said, ringing a bell to call in the maid. 'The phone, please, Joyce.'

'You really are spoilt rotten, you know,' Morgan said, finding a way to at least semi-lounge in the stiff chair.

Pamela only smiled. 'You should try it some time.'

CHAPTER NINE

THAT evening Saxon sat alone at a table in the semi-darkness of the after-hours Como Avenue shop. The golden glow of the luminous Bacio Bacio lightbox behind him gave him just enough light to read through the printout of the quarter's takings.

Though he wasn't looking at the page. He was leaning his chin on his palm and looking somewhere off into the distance. He was thinking of a million things—Sunday lunch, how well his dad was looking, Trisha seeming more and more bored every time he came to the shop as though it was beyond time he gave her more responsibilities. But it all somehow led back to one thing.

Her.

There was a knock at the front door. He blinked away the fog and lifted his head. The lights were off; the sign said closed. Some customers just didn't get it, did they?

His elbow took some time to straighten. How long had he been sitting there thinking? About her?

He held up a hand ready to point to the sign, when he recognised the outline of the person in the doorway.

The shape, the curves, the height, the wavy hair. And the itch. Oh, the itch! He could pick that silhouette from a crowd of a million.

He pulled himself from the chair and walked to the door. His blood warmed, his chest clenched harder with each step. His imagination went into overdrive as he pictured a sassy smile in Morgan's big green eyes, the delicious curve of her soft pink lips, the touch of her deft, artistic hands.

It staggered him that she made him feel like this from the other side of a door, in the dark, in his arms, any time, anywhere. The mere thought of her had him far more excited than figures and dollar signs and profits. She had him more excited than a twelve-year-old at Christmas.

He opened the door. She looked sexy as hell in a tight black and white jacket, skinny jeans, with an inch of tanned midriff showing beneath a tight white T-shirt. Designer-clad from top to toe. Meticulously tousled hair. Fingernails that took more time and effort than he took planning his whole day. And big beautiful eyes that made him think she carried the weight of the world on her small shoulders.

He'd spent a good part of the past hour imagining taking her right there on the terracotta-tiled floor. But seeing her in the flesh, he just wanted to hold her until she once again looked at him as she had looked at him when he'd found her lying naked on his bed the day before. Mellow, relaxed, happy.

But after the way they'd left things earlier that day he dared not. He stood back, as much as it pained him to do so, and let her set the mood.

She took a step inside, shuffling from one foot to the

other, and as the lightbox threw splashes of gold onto her face he saw more than restlessness in her eyes. He saw distress, regret, fear, desire, confusion. He saw so much emotion there he couldn't hope to keep up.

'Hi,' she said, glancing up at him quickly before looking away just as fast.

'Good evening.' His lazy words belied the tumult in his chest. 'I wasn't sure that I'd see you again. Tonight,' he added as an afterthought.

'Well, here I am.'

'Here you are.'

Here you are? Where was his usual cool? His infamous silver tongue? Probably the same place he'd left his every other part of himself that he still recognised—back on the day before she'd walked into his life. 'Did you find your car?'

'You were right. Towed,' she said, nodding. 'I paid the fine; they sent me another.'

'Very trusting of them.'

'They forgave me quick smart when I flashed my credit card and asked for an upgrade.'

He smiled as he was meant to do. Then he saw that she had his navy jumper in her hand. Gripped tight. As though she still needed an excuse to come see him and now that she'd clapped eyes on him she had forgotten she even had the thing.

This was a good sign. He wanted this woman making up excuses to see him. Or, better yet, admitting she wanted to see him without needing an excuse.

'Do you… Did you want a coffee?' he asked, moving deeper into the shop, into the glowing half-darkness.

She shook her head.

'No? You? Don't want a coffee?'

'I...' She blinked up at him, determination in her stance, in her eyes, before her shoulders shifted and she gave into temptation. 'Yeah, okay.'

That's my girl, he thought.

He moved behind the counter. She stood in the middle of the room just as she had that first day. Back then all he'd seen was a fun way to spend a lazy couple of days. Now he wanted to go back in time and slap himself up the back of the head for daring to think such thoughts about this woman.

He proceeded to make a skinny latte as he'd done a million times before. He could do it with his eyes closed as easily as a soldier could strip a gun.

When she caught him watching her instead she folded her arms, and then finally remembered the blue garment in her hand. 'I brought you this,' she said, holding it out to him. 'It's not laundered but—'

'Keep it.'

Her eyes flickered. Her cheek twitched and for a second he wasn't sure if she was about to smile, or about to cry. His heart stampeded through his chest.

'I don't think that's a good idea,' she said.

'It looked far better on you than it ever did on me.'

'I doubt that.'

He caught more than a hint of appreciation in her voice. *That's the spirit*, he thought. *Flirt. Bite back. Make me work for that gorgeous smile.*

Nevertheless she placed the folded jumper neatly on the table behind her.

Saxon glanced down before pouring the milk into the latte glass. He'd burnt himself once before by not watching that final step. The day Darius had told him his mum was on the phone, and his dad was in the hospital after the heart attack. It had left a scar. Far deeper than a shiny pink mark across his left knuckles. It was barely visible now. Did that tell him something? Had enough time passed for his inner scars to have healed as well?

Hell, yeah. His divorce had happened four years ago. He'd done a lot of living since that time. And a lot of learning. He'd paid his penance. His dad had given his blessing. He deserved a chance at something new, something real. The great question was: was Morgan ready to take the chance with him?

'This one's only half strength,' he said as he pushed it across the bench towards her. 'I don't want you to blame me for a lack of sleep tonight.'

He tried to grin, for he'd meant to remind her that she had no one to blame bar him for her lack of sleep the night before. But he just couldn't do it. The air felt heavy. His lips felt numb. Every word dropped like lead.

And this time when she walked to him and took her latte, he took the time to breathe in deep to relish her hot-cherry scent. His eyes roved over every inch of her, drinking her in. As though this might be his last chance.

He waited for her to look into the froth. She did. She held the glass with both hands and just stared into it. And in the place of the usual two x's, he'd carved two linked hearts.

The second she blinked down at the glass he wished he could take it back. It was cheesy. It was high-school-grade romance. It was the kind of thing some poor kid would do for his first true love. And he was better than that, more experienced than that.

Her big green eyes flickered up to meet his, and he knew in that moment he wasn't as experienced as he'd thought he was. This was a first. This feeling that he was teetering between hope and despair. He was wretchedly in love. For the first time in his whole life, he was truly, madly, deeply, smack-down, hit-to-the-head, sunken-guts, wildly-spinning-imagination, out-of-his-tree, out-of-his-depth in love.

Her eyes burned through him, branding him. Soul deep. All he could do was stare back, and hope that she took his gesture the right way: as a peace offering, a fresh start, a ray of hope that maybe, through all of this, they could forge a friendship. A relationship. A truly profound love affair that would stand the winds of change.

He could do this. She could do this. Together, united, they could do this…

She pushed the coffee back and took a step away and a rush of cool air slid in between them.

'Morgan,' he said, pulling up the barricade and walking to her.

She held up her hands and shook her head, her gorgeous waves settling over her shoulders.

'Don't do this, Morgan. There is absolutely no need to push me away. Last night was—'

'A mistake.'

'Amazing,' Saxon said at the same time.

Her chin shot an inch higher; her eyes were ablaze, hot, filled with desire, and more. He *knew* it. Yet he could still feel her pulling further away.

'It wasn't a mistake, Morgan. Don't you dare think that. It was the most brilliant night of my life. It beat my first kiss, it beat getting to first base with Maryanne Putney, it beat Italy winning the World Cup.' He shook his head. Now was not the time to be flippant. He wasn't wooing her, he was trying to tell her what she meant to him.

He caught up with her when the back of her knees hit the wrought-iron table. He reached out, ignoring the warning in her eyes, and ran a fast hand through her soft waves. 'Morgan, sweetheart, yesterday beat every day of my life before or since.'

She swallowed, her fine throat lifting and falling as her breaths grew to match his. 'But I came here…'

He smiled when she paused. 'To bring back my jumper, I know.' He moved his hand to cup her cheek. Her skin grew pink and patchy, her pupils dark and dreamy.

She blinked up at him, her eyes welling with confusion, and…love? A spark of heat lit him from within and travelled outward, melting away every last hard, sorry place inside him. He was ready for this. He was ready for her.

He trailed his hand deeper into her gorgeous hair. Her head fell back, ever so slightly, but just enough. Enough to tell him he wasn't alone in this crazy, unexpected flood of feelings that had swept him away.

He drew her closer against him, until her smooth curves found that perfect groove within his embrace.

And then he kissed her.

She didn't even pretend to not want it too. With a soft groan that had him growing hard in an instant she kissed him back. She clung to him, all yielding curves, sweet flavours, and yearning.

His hands slid beneath her jacket, needing to find skin, touch skin. He wrapped his arms beneath her tight T-shirt, the soft cotton holding him snug against her. She lifted to her tiptoes and it felt as though she wanted to climb inside him.

In a loud scrape of chairs against tiled floor he lifted her and walked her to a dark, hidden alcove in the corner of the room, where he pressed her back against the wall with a thud.

'Sorry,' he whispered.

'Don't be,' she said, then kissed him with so much heat he was lost again.

He pulled her jacket from her shoulders. Whipped her T-shirt over her head. Then his own sweater went the same way. He ran his hands over every inch of her beautiful glowing skin. His thumbs bumping over her dainty ribs. Sliding gently across the appendix scar above her hip-bone.

He kissed the top of her head. Her cheek. Her closed eyelids. He stroked her shoulder and she trembled. He slid her bra strap down until the delicate lace rolled away. He licked at the underside of her breast, then moved to take her hardening peak in his mouth.

She moaned. Slammed one hand against the wall and then slapped the other over her eyes. Her reaction triggered a surge of pure sexual energy sliding through him, rich and exotic.

He undid her fly, slid his hands into the back of her jeans, cupping her cheeks. She arched in pleasure, her head pressing against the wall, her hips pressing into his. Her hair fell off her shoulders in a great sexy swathe down her back.

He was so hard for her. Beyond ready. He wanted her so much he could barely see. She was just so…perfect. For him. Hard in the head and soft in his arms. So soft.

He slid her jeans from her slim legs, kicked off his own and paused, so close, so ready.

'Please,' she called out, her voice husky. For a second he thought she might be asking him to stop. If she did he might just cave in.

But then she nipped at the tight muscles of his shoulders and clawed the skin at his hips, dragging him inside her.

Her breath caught, once, twice as he slid deeper inside her. He felt her tighten around him and every pulse in his body throbbed, every muscle stretched, then constricted. The need to take her, to please her, to fill her was as sweet as tears.

The trip was smooth, silky, gorgeous. And when they hit their stride, when he felt her fall apart in his arms, Saxon let go. Completely and utterly at her mercy. The most intense pleasure of his lifetime drowning him in sensational waves. They clung to one another, until the swell abated.

The air around him settled until he heard the soft swoosh of cars driving by. The not-so-steady beat of her heart intermingling with the slightly slower, but no less heady beat of his own.

He needed her to know, to see, that this was no mistake. This was the opposite of a mistake. They were…meant to be. 'Morgan…'

'Shh,' she said, holding a finger to his lips, her voice wavering.

He kissed her fingertip and when she pulled it away he asked, 'What's wrong?'

She took a deep breath, gingerly slid her bra strap back over her shoulder to cover herself.

'Here.' Saxon grabbed her jacket from the table and slid it over her shoulders. She blinked up at him in thanks, but she didn't smile. Her soft lips had formed a thin horizontal line that made his stomach heave.

They dressed in silence. Silence so heavy it made his shoulders ache. His back. His heart. He needed to try to get through to her again. He reached out and touched her cheek. 'Morgan—'

'Saxon, I came here to tell you I've signed the papers with the investors. We're rebuilding Como Avenue. And I'm going home.'

'Home,' he repeated, somehow that last word piercing the deepest. His heart felt as if it were beating outside his chest.

'To Paris,' she said. 'Tonight.'

His thumb continued stroking her cheekbone as though it had a mind of its own and hadn't been rendered frozen by her announcement.

'You don't have to do that,' he said. Though he wasn't sure what he meant. Tear down his family business, or leave. Both? He wished he could rewind the clock and…what? Somehow save old man Kipling? But then she never would have come back and he never would have met her.

She pulled the edges of her jacket tighter around herself. 'I have a job. A life.'

'What kind of life?'

'A life I chose.'

'So choose again. It doesn't need to be this way.'

'It just *is* this way,' she said, her voice rising. Getting higher, louder, stronger. 'Whether I like it or not. You just refuse to see the problems. The reasons why this can't happen. Why I should have signed the damn plans back in Paris and just been done with it. It's like you're wearing magical blinkers or something.'

She buttoned up her jacket, and redressed hurriedly, running frantic fingers through her hair until it fell across her shoulders. A curtain. A shield.

'You can't hide from me, Morgan.'

'I don't hide. I'm not hiding. I could have just gone. I'm here, aren't I? Saying goodbye to your face.'

He knew then that she'd thought about it. She'd considered leaving and not saying goodbye. That hurt him more than he'd expected to be hurt ever again.

'You hide constantly,' he said. 'Behind your big sunglasses, your curtain of hair, your fancy clothes, your prickly personality. But don't you get it? I *see* you.'

He took a step towards her and pushed her hair away from her face as he'd done a dozen times before, knowing he wanted to do it a thousand times more. 'I *see* you, Morgan.'

She shook her head.

'You're a good person, Morgan. A person with so much heart. Such a beautiful heart.'

She closed her eyes shut tight and shook her head again. 'You can't know a person in four days. I've known people my whole life and never really known them.'

He placed a finger beneath her chin and tilted her head back up. 'I've come to know *you* in four days. And in that time you've come to know me too.'

Her bright green eyes flickered between his. Left to right. Hope warring against history. Desire fighting against her life story. She felt so right in his arms. Didn't she see that too? The rest…the rest was just choice and process.

She swallowed. 'My adult life has been spent believing survival means every girl for herself. And no matter how much it might appeal to do so, you can't change that in four days.'

Saxon didn't know what else he could say. The void between them suddenly looked so huge. He could no longer see all the way to the other side. And if he leapt now, and she wasn't there to catch him…

'My mother's husband is in property law,' she said. 'He has connections on the Heritage Council. They rejected your claim.'

'You've spoken to your mother?'

'I have.'

Wow, that was some step. If she could take that step, what was stopping her for from taking the next big leap?

'But that doesn't matter, Saxon. What matters is with one stroke of my pen I have gutted you and your family. You said it yourself. I'm the bad guy.'

'I was trying to annoy you.'

'I'm permanently annoyed, Saxon. You needn't have bothered.' She tilted her head. Her mouth even turned up at the corners a very little. And his heart leapt in his chest. She had absolutely no idea how sweet she really was. How kind, and empathetic, and caring.

Maybe she didn't want to be that way. Maybe she was scared of being hurt. Maybe she'd spent so long being tough and untouchable she couldn't find a way out of the mire. But so had he. And he was so close. So very close to being strong enough for both of them. 'Tell me you're not really going.'

'I'm not really going,' she said.

He laughed. Some of the tension eased. Some. But not much. For he knew what was holding him back that last inch. Why his toes clung onto the edge of the void with all their might. And her next words articulated it better than he ever could.

She let out a long slow sigh. 'Remember the day I took you away from your aunt's party? You still owe me for that. Now I'm asking you to pay up. *Let* me be the bad guy, Saxon. Tell your family you did everything you could, but I was an unpersuadable she-devil. Then spend your energy where it should be, cleaning up my mess.'

She was right. That was the hardest part. He just couldn't imagine sitting his parents down and telling them Como Avenue was lost, and the girl they'd told him to go forth and be fruitful with was the one who'd made it happen.

She looked at him then, really looked at him as though she was memorising the planes and angles of his face. Her eyes glowed with pain. At the thought of leaving him? Or was he merely projecting his own heartache. For that was what was happening as he felt her slipping out of his grasp. His heart physically hurt so that he needed to take deeper, slower breaths to keep his system working.

She picked up her T-shirt and his navy jumper. She held it out to him. He ignored it.

She drew in a sudden deep breath. Then leaned in and placed her small hand against his chest. Her touch was whisper-soft. She stood on her tiptoes and placed a kiss on his cheek. Her skin, her scent, wrapped around him, like a final touching embrace. It wasn't enough. It would never be enough.

When she pulled away she didn't look at him again. Head down, eyes averted. Was that a tear glimmering within? Too late. With a ding of the brass bell above the door, she was gone.

Saxon ran a hand over his stubbled chin. The scrape of sharp hair against the soft skin of his palm hurt. So he did it again. Anything to blot out the roar in his head as he felt her move further and further out of his life.

Her sweet curves, her mess of a hairstyle, her incomprehensible addiction to high fashion and dance music. He loved every single damn thing. For without even one of those specifics, she wouldn't be her. She wouldn't be the woman he loved.

As she walked past the window and out of view he noticed his jumper was still clutched in her hand. As though her subconscious didn't want her to let it go. To let him go.

He took a step forward, his heart pressing through his chest as though pointing the way. But his ego pulled him back in line.

For what did he know?

Maybe he could make a coffee like no one else. Maybe he had far more confidence than anyone had any right to have. Maybe she'd been waiting for him to make a grand gesture, to give her more than hot kisses and great sex.

But he let her go. For one talent he'd never managed to learn was the way to understand the vagaries of a woman's heart.

CHAPTER TEN

THE following day, Saxon shoved his cold hands into the pockets of his jeans and ambled down the windy, cracked, empty Como Avenue footpath to Jan's. Slowly.

For a blue envelope lay unopened in the office drawer back at Bacio Bacio. It had been delivered that morning. By registered post. Bearing the postmark of a city law office. He knew without even looking that it was his eviction notice. And he could only assume the others had left a message for him to join them at Jan's because they'd all received the same.

He'd already been to his parents' house early that morning. To tell them the news. To tell them the truth. The whole truth. About Barton, and Como Avenue. And about Morgan. And they had taken it far better than he had expected. They were upset. They were disappointed. They were even sad *for him*. But they bucked up and thanked God he had set up the company in such a way that no one store meant life or death for the label. And then they had gone about breakfast as before.

But he could in no way hope that the others would feel anywhere near the same way. He had failed them, just as he'd failed his family years before. For the sake of a woman. A woman he'd understandably fallen for but mistakenly trusted. Trusted to do the right thing by him.

He stood outside Jan's and wrapped his hand around the old brass handle, the cold metal burning into his palm. Then he let go and looked at his reflection in the curtained window, outlined against the bright blue winter sky.

'Stop feeling so bloody sorry for yourself, mate,' he said. 'She did the right thing by *herself*. What more could you really have expected her to do? Seriously. Now go in there and tell *them* that. They may turn on you for it, but the dismal truth is you love her. And she's not here to defend herself. Right? So be a man and go to it.'

He thumped himself in the chest, sniffed deep through his nose. And when he opened the door to hear laughter coming from within, he stood back and checked he had the right place.

'Saxon!' Morris called out.

'Hi, guys,' Saxon said from the doorway. To a one they were smiling, grinning, pink-cheeked, and each and every one of them held a glass of champagne.

He wondered for a second, for one brief beautiful second, if the night before had been some kind of dream. The sex had been so phenomenal it could easily have been all in his head. Maybe the rest had been too. 'What am I missing here?' he asked.

'Don't act all coy, buddy boy,' Morris said, flapping his hand to encourage Saxon inside. 'We know we have you to thank.'

'You want to thank me?' Okay, so maybe *this* was the dream. Right now. No tears, no shirt-tugging, no pleas that he track the woman down and wring her neck for the good of the avenue…

'He doesn't know. Show him, Cassie,' Jan said from behind her nearly-empty glass of champagne.

Cassie Chang lifted a piece of paper from the desk. It was pale blue. This wasn't a dream.

'We are being shut down, are we not?' he asked.

Jan nodded and smiled. Morris, rosy cheeks, beamed. The Purans giggled into their champagne flutes.

'With two hundred thou in our pockets, we are!' Adele said, getting up off her stool to do a little jig. 'Oh, happy day!'

Saxon blinked. 'Did you just say two hundred thousand dollars?'

'Each business,' Cassie said. 'Relocation costs, they called them.'

'And they've ordered half of my bloody shop for the interiors of the new beautiful building they plan on erecting atop our ashes,' Jan said, her blue eyes bright with adventure. 'If this was what we were in for we should have let the old man tear this dump down years ago.'

'So you're okay. You're all okay.'

'We will be now,' Adele said, blinking up at him with tears in her eyes. 'Thanks to you.'

Saxon held up his hands. 'No, no, no. This had nothing to do with me. Or Barton Kipling, I can promise you that. This was all Morgan. She came up with this all on her own. Without a lick of support from me.'

'Sure,' Morris said, slapping him on the back. 'Whatever you say.'

'No, truly. She thought of you, made sure to look out for you, all on her own. I just can't imagine how.'

And why hadn't she mentioned any of this the night before? Oh, he knew how! And there he had been, the night before, telling her he *saw* her. When he hadn't really seen her fully until this moment. Morgan loved him right on back. He'd seen it in her eyes, felt it in her embrace, tasted it in her kisses. Only history had made it far too hard for her to love herself enough to believe that if she took the leap out into the great abyss anybody would truly be there to catch her.

Saxon felt his toes uncurl, and the itch was back. But this itch was in his feet. And it was telling him to get moving, towards the cause. And fast.

'I am thinking of opening up another Punjabi Palace closer to home,' Ignatius Puran said, moving on already.

'We are thinking of playing the stock markets for a while, then retiring,' Cassie Chang said.

'And what about you?' Morris asked.

Saxon was listening, but his mind was already miles away. He was packing his high-school French phrase book. Shuffling through his home-office drawer for his passport. Tucking Morgan's business card into his wallet. He was throwing Darius and Trisha in the deep end and giving them the reins of the business while he went away for a while.

'Going somewhere, Saxon?' Jan asked before he'd even taken a breath.

Saxon backed towards the door. 'Yeah. Yeah I am.'

Morgan walked from the *Châtelet* metro station, along the edge of the Seine to the *Chic* offices, hidden beneath the shade of a parasol to fend off the sun. Summer in Paris had hit hot and sticky. It was so bright she struggled to keep her eyes open even behind her huge sunglasses.

It didn't much help that she hadn't slept all that well since coming back. She put it down to the fact that the tourist season had hit with a vengeance and the Montmartre nightlife was in full swing.

And the fact that she had blithely walked away from the only man she had ever loved. All right, so it hadn't been in any way blithe. It had been hard. And painful. But she didn't regret it. Couldn't. There was no way she could have rubbed his family's nose in what she had done by staying any longer. Leaving was her last act of love. *Ever.*

She tucked her new favourite handbag, a vintage clutch purse she'd picked up the day before for three Euros at a flea market, beneath her arm, and swerved to avoid the dog droppings scattering the footpath.

She smiled at the doorman as he opened the door for her. He tipped his hat. He'd worked in the building for over two years and she realised she had no idea what his name was, neither he hers.

'*Je suis Morgan,*' she said, holding out her hand.

'*Charles,*' he countered, affording her a huge grin and a pleasant handshake.

A slight lift to her mood, she hopped into the beautiful old elevator, pulled shut the door, then the grate and pressed the decorative button for the fourth floor, and watched the hand turn as it winched slowly skyward. Towards the *Chic* offices.

And while she had managed to keep herself busy enough these last couple of days, revisiting her favourite places in Paris, eating at her favourite restaurants, standing on her balcony and drinking in the beauty of the Sacre Coeur for hours each night, the closer she got to work, the more her stomach felt as if it had been left on the ground floor.

Today she was meant to be dressing a set for a shoot in the elegant and beautiful Hôtel Biron, surrounded by the collected works of Rodin. It had taken her three months to convince the estate she was going to treat the gardens with respect. And while she had been away Alicia had changed the tweed, jodhpurs and riding boots spread into fluorescent leggings and white plastic belts in some kind of eighties retrospective.

She bit her lip. She needed this job, now more than ever. After the way she had handled the Como Avenue debacle, this was all she had. All she would ever have. It had been enough for her a week ago. It would *have* to be enough for her now.

Enough. The word landed in her subconscious like a fat stone in a shallow pond. Could enough ever really be enough? After she'd tasted more. After she'd experienced everything. For one beautiful day in the mountains with Saxon, she'd seen what life had on offer for those brave enough to allow intimacy and love into their lives…

The lift juddered to a halt. She blinked at her reflection in the shiny art-deco doors. The grate spilt her image into a hundred different parts. Which was pretty much how she felt right about then.

'No more of that,' she said out loud. 'No more.'

She sniffed in deep through her nose. Then she sniffed again when she realised she could smell cinnamon on the air. She closed her eyes, and in a burst of pure indulgence sniffed long, and hard, and deep as the scent enveloped her. Taking her back, across an ocean and into Saxon's arms…

'Morgan, sweetie!'

She opened her eyes and jumped in fright. The lift

doors were open and her assistant stood before her, carrying a cup of coffee, no doubt for himself, and twirling a hot pink tassel around his finger.

'Leon. Good morning,' she said as she shot past him and down the hall towards her desk.

Leon jogged to catch up. 'So are you really back for good?'

'I'm really back for good,' she said. No retirement. No starting her own business. No moving anywhere ever again unless she won the lottery. 'Sorry. You can't have my job. Or my desk. Or my coffee mug.'

She reached out and grabbed it out of his hand and took a great long gulp. It was good. But it wasn't great. It wasn't smooth, and hot, and strong with a kick that made her skin tingle. Was she going to have to give up coffee as well as designer clothes in order to forget about Saxon?

'Here,' she said, giving it back. 'You can have my mug. I should be drinking more water anyway.'

'Thanks. Now, I'm just asking about you coming or going because, you kind of have someone—'

Morgan rounded the partition to find a large male form decked out in leather and denim sitting on the corner of her desk, flicking through the previous month's copy of *Chic*. His dark hair was too long. His shoulders so broad. And he smelt of so very much like cinnamon.

'—here to see you,' Leon finished, waving at her visitor as is he were the prize on a game show.

She was dreaming. Surely that was the only possible meaning behind this vision. She was so tired, and so lovesick, that she had conjured him as some kind of hallucination.

Saxon spun around. And the moment her eyes met his she knew it was no dream. Her knees gave way.

Leon squealed and leapt backward.

But Saxon's reflexes were much better. Or maybe he'd been expecting it. Either way he reached out and caught her by the elbows. Once she was upright, he slid her purse from under her arm and put it behind him, his eyes not leaving hers. He hooked her parasol over the back of her chair. And then slowly, slowly slid her large sunglasses off her nose.

Without the dark shield he looked even better. Bigger. More real. She could see the golden flecks in his warm brown eyes. The touch of a smile on his beautiful lips. And new creases in his wide forehead.

Before she knew she was about to do it, she reached up and ran a finger along their grooves. It had been three days—or was it four?—since she'd seen him last. And she could see the differences in him. She knew his face that well. No matter how hard she'd tried to deny it she *saw* him.

He reached out and tucked a hand beneath her hair, sliding his palm along her neck. Her eyes fluttered closed and she leant her head sideways, snuggling against his touch. It just felt so good, so right, as if it had been months, years, a lifetime since he'd touched her last.

'Shall I leave you two alone?' Leon asked.

Morgan's eyes fluttered open. She'd forgotten where she was. And who else was there.

'What do you think?' Saxon said, his voice gruff.

Leon took off at a trot, no doubt to tell the office everything about Morgan and her dashing Australian friend who had followed her all the way to Paris.

Saxon stood, his broad form and masculinity swamping her. 'Can we…?' he began before clearing his throat. 'Can we maybe go for a walk?'

The clock on the wall said she was late already. She had a meeting with the whole editorial team in ten minutes. Where Alicia would no doubt announce that next week's shoot at Le Procope, the world's first café, a place where Napoleon had planned battles, and now one of Paris's most beautiful restaurants, would now need to be decked out with a fluorescent sportswear theme.

A choice was upon her. To stay, go to her meeting, keep her head down and not rock the boat and keep her tragic job. Or go with Saxon for a walk, risking further damage to her already-far-too-bruised heart, risking Alicia's neurotic ire, and finding out why he was here.

Had his family kicked him out of town after having had enough of his taste in women? Had the Como Avenue gang sent him as their emissary to plead with her to change her mind?

Or had he come back for his jumper? She should have posted it back. Or left it with the concierge to deliver for her. But she'd kept it. And as it was too hot to wear it, she used it as a pillow every night since she'd returned to her tiny apartment. She'd hugged it to herself. And she'd fallen asleep not long before dawn. Because she was in love with him. She'd gone but she couldn't let him go. And now he was here. He was really *here*. Who was she kidding? Her choice had been made the moment she'd smelt cinnamon in the lift.

'Sure, let's go,' she said, grabbing her sunnies and her purse. She moved in a circle, then turned and moved in a circle again. Not suite sure which way to go. He had her rattled.

She took a slightly calming breath and led him back into the lift. He pulled the grate closed. She pressed the button for the ground floor. Their eyes met and they both smiled politely.

The scent of his cinnamon, and his old leather jacket, wrapped around her in the confined space. So she kept her eyes dead ahead. And breathed through her mouth.

The lift hit ground level. The doors opened. Alicia bundled in with her shih-tzu tucked under her arm; the dog was wearing an outfit that matched her own.

'Bienvenue en arrière.'

Welcome back, Morgan translated. Not welcome *home*.

'Maintenant, up up up we go,' Alicia demanded.

Saxon headed out of the lift. But Morgan's feet were rooted to the spot. It was as though two paths had opened up beneath her feet. One leading up and one leading out. The decision was now. Here. Either way there would be no turning back.

She stared at Saxon who stood in the doorway. Watching. Waiting. Patiently. Smiling. As though he truly trusted her to make the right decision.

'Morgan. Up up!' Alicia repeated, stubbornly waiting for someone else to do the hard work of closing the grate.

Morgan facilitated her. She stepped out of the lift and closed the grate on Alicia's shocked face. This time Saxon pressed the button to send the lift upward.

'Well, that was far too much fun,' Morgan said, feeling giddy. As if she'd swallowed a whole canister of helium.

'Shall we?' Saxon said, holding out his hand. She slid hers inside his, relishing the warmth and texture.

So familiar. So enticing. She shivered under his touch, and she saw the moment he knew it. His eyes grew dark, and his smile grew bigger.

'*Charles,*' she said, nodding at the doorman who let them out, and this time when he tipped his cap he gave her a wink.

When they hit the street outside she turned and started walking, nerves finally hitting as the two of them were to all intents and purposes alone for the first time since she had loved him and left him and put his flagship store out of business.

She pretended to pay close attention to the florists' and pet stores on her right fighting for space while creating a truly unique mix of scents. To her left street vendors selling prints and oils and second-hand books blocked the view of the Seine. While all the while she wished they were back at Mt Buller, in the cold and the snow, wrapped in one another's warm embrace, before everything had somehow gone horribly wrong.

'I love this part of town,' she said after thirty seconds of painful silence. 'Pretty, don't you think?'

'It's lovely.'

She glanced across to find him watching her. Her pulse beat hard and fast in her throat. God, it was good to see him. But it would be far better for her rampaging heart rate if she knew why he'd wanted to see her. There was only one way to find out. 'Why are you here, Saxon?'

'I want you to tell me why I didn't get the two-hundred-grand payout like the rest of them.'

Well, so much for, *I missed you, come home.*

Embarrassment mixed with frustration. He hadn't tried to kiss her, or hold her close. Maybe she'd read him all wrong. Maybe she'd hurt him too much, and he'd come here to give her a piece of his mind. She tugged her hand from his and used it to jab a finger into her palm. 'First, I hoped you might still accept my offer of a spot in the new precinct. Second, you don't need the money. And third, well, I didn't want it to seem like some kind of payment of services rendered.'

At that Saxon finally broke down and laughed. He stopped walking, put his hands to his knees, stood in the middle of the bustling footpath and laughed. She backed up, grabbed him by the elbow and kept him moving, turning him down a graded path to the bank of the Seine so he wouldn't get in anybody else's way.

'If you are here for the money…' she began, though she didn't really want to finish. For there was pretty much none left.

'I'm not,' he said. He placed his spare hand over hers and locked his elbow to his side so that she had to walk flush up against him. He slowed his pace as well, and he was so much bigger than her she had no choice but to slow too.

Cobblestones disappeared beneath her feet. Weeping willows dipped their bright summer leaves into the water as though taking a drink. Water lapped at the edge of the path as a riverboat sailed by, tourists waving at the couples promenading. Morgan did not wave back.

'I assume the money came from the investors,' he said.

She thought about how much that would be giving away, then nodded.

'Well, it worked a charm. Last I heard the Purans and the Changs were discussing starting up some crazy fusion restaurant. Morris is in Queensland already.

Something about a water park he's always wanted to see. And Jan has some ideas about which of her fabrics might in fact make fabulous-dressing room curtains. Won't make a decision without you, though. How did you pull it off?'

'I can be pretty persuasive when I want to be,' she said.

'No,' he said, laughing again, 'you really can't. Your temper is far too short. I can't for the life of me figure out the deal you made.'

'It doesn't really matter. What's important is that this way everyone is happy as they can possibly be under the circumstances.'

'Except you,' he said, looking down into her eyes. She used her spare hand to shield her face from the sun, and refused to look at him. The tenderness in his voice was far too much to bear. 'You came back here, and let the opportunity of a lifetime pass you by back in Melbourne.'

'I have a highly sought-after job here, Saxon. There's no point in throwing all that away for a one-off project that never really should have been mine in the first place.'

They passed through a tunnel beneath one of Paris's famous bridges, and Morgan lowered her hand. Saxon slowed to a halt in its cool shadows. He waited until her eyes skittered up to meet his. Dark, deep, reflecting just the slightest glint off the nearby river. 'I didn't mean the shops, Morgan. I meant me.'

If she'd thought her heart had been racing earlier she'd had no idea. It now did a kind of quickstep in her chest. 'You have some kind of arrogance, Saxon Ciantar,' she said, trying for strong and sassy, but her wavering voice gave her away.

'Not arrogance,' he said, running the back of his finger down her cheek, so softly her eyes fluttered closed. 'Confidence. It comes from being right all the time.'

'Right?' she repeated on a whisper, her eyes fluttering open again.

He slowly wrapped his arms about her waist, drawing her to him. And she let him. Wanton hussy that she was, she melted into him the first chance she had, letting her arms rest flat against his chest, her knee slide against his knee. Boy, did it feel good.

'All the time. And you know what else I'm right about? You offered Bacio Bacio a spot in that new precinct of yours because you want *me* there. You don't even like gelato. There's no point in denying it any longer, Morgan Kipling-Rossetti. You are *so* into me.'

She pushed back, mostly so that he couldn't tell that her heart was making shapes against her ribs. 'You think I didn't give you two hundred thousand dollars of my own money because I'm *into* you? What are you, like, sixteen?'

'Hang on,' he said, his cheeky smile evaporating in the blink of an eye. 'That was your own money?'

Her cheeks pinked, while she tried to look anywhere but into those beautiful, empathetic, knowing brown eyes. But she had no chance. For those eyes were like magnets to hers.

'Well, no,' she said, blinking profusely. 'Not exactly. I mean, I had to set a price for the land now, and in nine years the relocation money will come out of my profits. That's the only way I could get them to agree to the payout now. But that's okay. As I see it the money never really was mine.'

He let her go and began to pace. Two steps one way. Two steps the other. 'You nutty, hot-headed woman. That's the last piece of advice I would have given you. You don't take yourself down with a sinking ship. You deserve better than that.'

She crossed her arms and glared at him. 'What makes you think I would have done one thing you told me to do?'

He shook his fists at the dark, dank underside of the bridge. 'Aah! You drive me so crazy!'

'Well, right back at you.'

'And you know what else?'

He stopped pacing and grabbed her by the upper arms, so suddenly she just blinked up at him and said, 'What?'

Then with a primal growl he pulled her to him, and kissed her as though his life depended on it. She stood there and took it. Closed her eyes shut tight and let him.

It felt as if it were her first kiss. Ever. It was shocking. Sweet. Tender. Erotic. And just wonderful. Within moments she felt as if she were drifting five inches above the ground.

His hands shifted to tuck beneath the weight of her hair, gentle pressure turning her head ever so slightly so that their lips could meet more fully. More deeply.

Unable to keep herself steady, she leant against him and slid her arms around his waist. Her limbs turning slack the moment she had his hot, hard body to rest on.

When he finally pulled away, he leant his forehead against hers. His breaths were ragged. Hers too. She took a short breath, ready to tell him why, when he placed a finger against her mouth.

'Morgan, I love you,' he said before she could even protest. She let her breath out slowly through her nose

as his words sank in. 'I love you so much I don't care
that you're pulling down my shop. I know how you
struggled to make that decision. How hard I made it on
you to make that decision alone. And how I never want
you to have to go through anything like that alone again.
Any day alone. Any moment.'

Saxon lifted his head, shook back his hair and
watched her for several long, beautiful, breathtaking
seconds, as though he needed time for a thousand
thoughts to coagulate into one.

He pushed her hair off her face, so that there was
nowhere left to hide, even if she'd wanted to. 'I love that
you make me feel permanently off balance. I love that
your mouth always kicks into the slightest smile just
before I kiss you. I love that your hair always looks like
you've just rolled out of bed. I love the little mole
beneath your eye, and your unbelievably sexy red
toenails, and the way you fit against me when you lie
wrapped in my arms. And most of all I absolutely love
your beautiful, kind, wide-open heart.'

He pulled her hand to cover his own heart. It was
beating as hard and fast as her own.

And Morgan couldn't find one thing to say. Her
words were caught in a knot in her throat. Her emotions
running away from her, out of her control. But she knew
in that moment she didn't want to control them. She
wanted to simply be, and feel, and let them wash over
her. For it felt just beautiful.

He leaned down and kissed her again. Softly.
Sweetly. A kiss that took her far away from Paris and
the cobblestone street beneath her feet. His warm lips,
his singular sweet taste, his strong embrace took her
back to hazy days spent with him in Melbourne.

Summer dropped away and the only warmth she felt was in his arms. He took her home.

His kiss slowed and her feet touched the ground once more. 'You could have done that ten minutes ago, you know,' she said. 'Would have saved a lot of bother.'

He grinned. 'And a heck of a lot of fun too.'

He loosened his grip. Just enough that he could lean back and look into her eyes. Her breath heaved in and out, creating such a happy ache in the region of her heart. For in that moment she knew he truly saw her. He saw her and he loved her.

Morgan swallowed down the lump that threatened to lodge tight in her throat once more. No more holding back. No more lack of faith. No more fear. She felt two fat tears trail down her cheeks as she said the words she'd never thought would ever leave her mouth, her heart. 'Saxon, I love you.'

'I know,' he said, reaching out and wiping her tears away with gentle thumbs.

'I mean I really, truly love you.' She was getting the hang of this now. 'Leaving you that night was the hardest thing I've ever done my whole life. But I had to. I thought I was doing the right thing by you.'

'I *know*,' he said, laughing. 'It's okay. I know.'

He slid his arm around her waist and tucked her tight against him as he continued strolling with her along the beautiful bank of the beautiful Seine. 'So, anyway, I was thinking maybe we could spend a week here. Two, even. To give you a chance to convince me that this place has anything over Melbourne apart from a tall tower. Before we head home.'

Home. He wanted her to come home. To a place where people knew her name. Where people loved her.

Where she planned on having a lot of say in the interior design of what would be the best new shopping precinct Carlton had ever seen. And where the opportunity of a lifetime was awaiting her.

'So you're not going to move here to be with me?' she asked, tongue firmly planted in cheek.

The thought of leaving Leon to look after the plastic belts and fluorescent stockings, spending two weeks saying goodbye to a city that had taken her in with open arms when she'd needed them most, then heading home to freezing cold nights wrapped in Saxon's arms was far too fabulous to resist.

'You are one cheeky miss,' he said. 'Don't ever change.'

He kissed her on her nose, then seemed to realise that would never be enough so he drew her to him, bent her back and gave her a Hollywood kiss, hard on the mouth, to the enjoyment of a passing pair of joggers who shouted out their best wishes in rather risqué French.

'What did they say?' Saxon murmured against her mouth.

She laughed and forced him to bring her upright. 'How about I show you when we find ourselves a nice comfy bed?'

'Right.' At that Saxon picked her up and threw her over his shoulder and started jogging in the direction of his hotel.

She screamed at him to put her down, but was laughing so hard she made no sense.

'One thing,' he said, slowing and sliding her back down his front until she found herself desperately hoping his hotel was a hell of a lot closer than her apartment. 'I am going to need my navy jumper back.'

'Never,' she said, wrapping her fingers around the hair at the base of his neck. 'Think of it as payment for services about to be rendered.'

'I truly don't know what I'm going to do with you, Morgan Kipling-Rossetti,' Saxon murmured, sending shivers of anticipation shooting up her spine.

'Love me,' she said, the words leaving her breathless. Beautifully, beautifully breathless. 'Just love me.'

'That,' he said, 'won't be a problem.'

And then he kissed her. And, boy, was her man talented.

EPILOGUE

THE grand opening of the new Rossetti on Como shopping strip went off without a hitch.

The summer sun shone. Crowds clogged the street. And the press were out in force, especially when they all heard that the new two-storey Bacio Bacio flagship store would be giving away free gelato to all that day.

Morgan stood back and watched it all unfold from a distance. She wrapped her arms around her stomach, hugging close the happy feelings she was still getting used to feeling every day.

A pair of warm, strong arms slid around her waist from behind, and the happy feelings blew wide open.

'Hey there, stranger,' she said.

Saxon nuzzled against her neck. 'How much longer is this going to be? I'm starved. And you taste amazing. Do you always taste this amazing? I'm sure I would remember if you *always* tasted this amazing.'

'Oh, shush,' she said. 'Mum's about to cut the ribbon.' He stopped talking but he continued nuzzling, while Morgan tried her best to pay attention to the festivities while her toes curled and her stomach turned to molten heat. Six months in and he still made her feel crazy in lust with one touch. One look. One press of his long, hard form against her back.

'Saxon,' she murmured. 'The ribbon.'

'Fine,' he said, ceasing nuzzling. 'It'll wait.'

A huge pink sash wrapped all the way around the two-storey edifice had been attached by guys in cherry pickers that morning. She'd thought it a little over the top when her mum had suggested it, but now she was glad she'd done it. It looked fabulous and people would be talking about it for days.

'Are you entirely certain that woman is your mother?' Saxon asked.

Pamela, looking resplendent in brand-new pink Chanel to match the ribbon, shed a tear or two as she talked about how much her husband, an architect himself, would have been so proud of his daughter for bringing to life such a landmark building.

Morgan leaned back into his embrace. 'I'm afraid so. Before she had hers done we had the exact same nose.'

She tilted her head back and grinned up at her gorgeous man. He leaned over her and kissed the tip of her nose. 'I like yours better.'

She snuggled in tighter. 'Lucky for me. So what do you think?'

'I think it's time someone appeared from the sidelines with a great big hook and dragged her away.'

She pinched his arm. 'I mean of our building.'

He dropped his chin to land atop her head. 'It's a beautiful building. It brought your family back together. And it brought us together period. Being that he was an architect, a father and a Frenchman, I think your dad would have been really proud of you on all counts.'

She sighed. 'He would have loved this.'

He wrapped his arms tighter around her still. 'And not to mention what it's done for the old Como gang. Have you seen Morris Cosgrove? He's lost at least thirty pounds and he's almost as tanned as George Hamilton!'

Morgan tilted her head where the old inhabitants of Como Avenue were standing in a small group. They all looked well. And happy. And collectively about a hundred years younger.

'I did the right thing, then?'

'Sure. You did a great thing. Though I'm not sure that loving and marrying me is really a *smart* thing.'

She spun in his arms and grinned up at him. 'I know the past few months have been hectic but I don't remember any kind of ceremony happening in between times.'

'Right,' he said, nodding as though she'd shown him the light. 'I'd forgotten.'

She just laughed. They had joked about it a thousand times. Once they'd returned to Melbourne life had simply happened around them and they had just gone on loving one another. Their friends joked they acted like honeymooners anyway. And she was perfectly happy with that. She trusted the strength of his love implicitly. She had no idea how she managed it, she just did. And she was forever grateful.

She sent up a small prayer of thanks to her father for giving her the genes to be able to love this way. And for good measure another small prayer of thanks to her grandfather, wherever he was, for unwittingly giving her the greatest gift a granddaughter could ever want: a family of her own.

'Ooh,' Saxon said, taking her by the hand and dragging her through the crowd. 'Food's up.'

The invited guests headed indoors to the Red Windmill, a new French restaurant on the ground floor—Morgan had designed the interior, giving it an opulent Moulin Rouge feel—where a lavish celebratory buffet awaited them.

Cassie Chang lifted her feet carefully as she walked up the red carpet snaking through the middle of the centre, not wanting to leave a mark. Adele clung tight to the arm of her new boyfriend, a guy ten years younger than her who hung off her every word. Jan pointed out to anyone who would listen which soft furnishings had at one time been hidden in the bottom of an old crate in her storeroom.

Once everyone was seated and eating, Saxon took Morgan's hand and pulled her to her feet, then clinked his spoon against the side of a champagne glass.

Still not used to being the centre of anybody's attention, Morgan picked up a canapé and a glass of champagne and continued to eat and drink as Saxon spoke.

'I'd like to make a toast,' he said. 'To my beautiful Morgan and her beautiful new building.'

'To Morgan—' the gang began.

She waved the hand with the canapé across her face. 'Stop the gushing. It's not my building. I consider myself a caretaker. From one old man to a whole group of old men this building shall pass.'

'Not so,' Saxon said.

She lifted her eyes to his.

'As of about three o'clock yesterday afternoon. The investors have been paid back every penny they have outlaid thus far. Plus interest. Rossetti on Como is officially now in the hands of a Rossetti as it is meant to be. My gift, my sweet, to you.'

Morgan gaped. Gaped and swallowed as a river of tears threatened to fall. But Saxon wasn't done yet.

'Now,' he said, 'where was I? Ah, that's right. I'd like you all to raise your glasses to my beautiful bride, Morgan—'

'He's kidding,' she said to the table at large, before saving a glare for him. 'It's this in joke we have, because we're always so busy and…'

Saxon sank down onto one knee in front of her friends and family and all the crazy Melbournites she loved, and her words turned to fresh air.

She stared at him, a canapé in one hand, a glass of champagne in the other. It took for her mother to reach across and take them from her and give her a little shove in Saxon's direction.

She took his hand. It was trembling. They both were trembling. He brought out a small black velvet box and opened it to reveal…her mother's first engagement ring.

Her blurry gaze shot to her mother, who had her hands clasped tight together as she smiled at her through a wave of tears. And nodded.

Morgan sniffed and looked back to Saxon. The love of her life. Her dream come true.

'Morgan Kipling-Rossetti, I want to marry you. You know that. Everyone knows that. I just wanted everyone to know that I've set the date. One month from now. Right here. With all of these people as our guests. What do you think?'

'I think I'm going to cry all over your beautiful new jacket if you say another word. And yes. Yes, of course, a thousand times yes.'

She threw herself into his arms, and the table exploded in a round of applause.

'One condition,' he whispered against her ear.

She pulled back to look into his beautiful eyes. 'Anything.'

'If I have to become Saxon Kipling-Rossetti-Ciantar then I take it all back.'

She laughed. 'We'll see,' she said, leaning in for a kiss. 'I am quite the persuader, you know.'

THE ROYAL HOUSE OF NIROLI

*...International affairs, seduction
and passion guaranteed*

VOLUME FOUR

The Tycoon's Princess Bride
by Natasha Oakley

Isabella Fierezza has always wanted to make a
difference to the lives of the people of Niroli and she's
thrown herself into her career. She's about to close
a deal that will ensure the future prosperity of the
island. But there's just one problem...

Domenic Vincini: born on the neighbouring, *rival*
island of Mont Avellana, and he's the man who can
make or break the deal. But Domenic is a man with
his own demons, who takes an instant dislike to
the perfect Fierezza princess...

*Worse, Isabella can't be in the same room with him –
without wanting him! But if she gives in to temptation,
she forfeits her chance of being queen...and will tie
Niroli to its sworn enemy!*

Available 5th October 2007

www.millsandboon.co.uk

THE ROYAL HOUSE OF NIROLI

...International affairs, seduction and passion guaranteed

Volume 5 – November 2007
Expecting His Royal Baby by Susan Stephens

Volume 6 – December 2007
The Prince's Forbidden Virgin by Robyn Donald

Volume 7 – January 2008
Bride by Royal Appointment by Raye Morgan

Volume 8 – February 2008
A Royal Bride at the Sheikh's Command by Penny Jordan

8 volumes in all to collect!

Mediterranean Men

Let them sweep you off your feet!

Gorgeous Greeks

The Greek Bridegroom by Helen Bianchin
The Greek Tycoon's Mistress by Julia James
Available 20th July 2007

Seductive Spaniards

At the Spaniard's Pleasure by Jacqueline Baird
The Spaniard's Woman by Diana Hamilton
Available 17th August 2007

Irresistible Italians

The Italian's Wife by Lynne Graham
The Italian's Passionate Proposal by Sarah Morgan
Available 21st September 2007

www.millsandboon.co.uk